Grimoires and Green Tea

A Woodside Cosy Urban Fantasy

Melissa Gunn

ROSE KOWHAI PRODUCTIONS

Edited by Grace Bridges

Cover and interior design by Melissa Gunn

ISBN Ebook 978-1-06704-618-7

ISBN paperback 978-1-06704-619-4

ISBN hardcover 978-1-0670967-0-0

ISBN audiobook 978-1-0670967-1-7

Contents

For Zelda, who sat with me while I wrote this book, and only sometimes begged for treats.

Chapter One

THE BOOKSHOP

Waking up in my new apartment over a magical bookshop was a luxurious feeling. No distant lowing of cows or bleating of sheep. No early-morning alarm reminding me to check the daily financial papers in time for the morning pre-scrying briefing. No family expectations of how to behave, what to eat, how to spend my day. By the Oracle, what would I do? The possibilities were endless. Best of all, no-one would tell me what was going to happen before it actually did. It *was* a shame that I'd woken up with the smell of wood smoke suffusing my nostrils, reminding me of the previous day's adventure.

Faced with a bewildering array of options and no authority figure with instructions, decision paralysis kept me in bed for another fifteen minutes. But hunger got me up in the end. Hunger, and the desire to be rid of the smell of smoke.

I'd packed a couple of snacks, but I was in the city now. Didn't cities have cafes? Would they be open at... I looked around for my phone to check the time and located it halfway under the bed, fortunately still plugged in. I frowned as I hauled it up by its cord. Surely I'd left it last night on the convenient bedside table that was part of the apartment's furniture? I didn't think I was that much of an active sleeper. But the phone assured me I had time to find something for breakfast even if I did decide to open the shop today.

What a daunting prospect. Maybe tomorrow is soon enough. Or next week. In fact, I probably need a marketing campaign first.

I'd spent the evening munching on trail mix and browsing through the bookshelves, but I hadn't really got the basics of retail operation sorted out in my head yet, let alone being ready to try it for real. Still, I couldn't put off opening the shop for too long; after all, Kath had told me that I could have the shop so long as I kept it running.

I had a long shower—washing my long chestnut hair with no-one hurrying me out of it so they could have their turn, and town water supply, so no running out of tank water, what bliss!—and dressed in the second of three outfits I'd decided were worth bringing with me. I glanced down at myself, clad in soft trousers and a T-shirt. *Would I stick out, showing my rural origins? Should I have opted for something more feminine?* But I wanted to be comfortable today. I expected to be moving a lot of books.

Oh well, I can always buy more clothes. Once I've figured out this magical bookshop business, at least. You'll be fine, Sibyl, I reassured myself.

Was it only yesterday I'd left home looking for a future that *wasn't* foreseen by my Seer family? (A bit late, some might say, since I was already in my late twenties). Actually, they'd probably see my future whatever I did. Seers, you know. But as someone who'd failed the sibylline exams required to become a Seer myself, I was keen to put as much distance as possible between me and a future I wasn't cut out for, working (unsuccessfully) to predict financial futures. Not that my family was unsuccessful in their predictions—that was just me. I'd used as much education and statistical analysis as I could in my attempt to fit in with the family business, but it simply hadn't worked.

I'd moved out of home in what some would call a bit of a rush, trying to minimise the predictive abilities of my family by making snap decisions—not my usual approach to life at all. But I wanted to strike out and find out what I could do by myself, away from my all-Seeing family.

Fortunately, my shower meant I no longer smelt of wood smoke. Once the steam had evaporated from the mirror in the bathroom, I combed my hair and put on my glasses so I could assess my appearance. Wavy hair, flattened and darkened from the shower. Check. Silver-grey eyes that suggested a Seeing ability I didn't possess. Check. Average nose, average mouth, average face. Check. I was ready to see the world. Or at least the city. Maybe just the bookshop.

The bus I'd taken at random yesterday (well, as much at random as possible in a small rural town with only the long-distance inter-city buses stopping there) had taken me on an unexpectedly eventful journey. I'd survived the bus ride itself, something which hadn't felt guaranteed at some points of the trip. I'd met werewolves. I'd even escaped death by dragon (of the small, swampy variety)! That was an experience I wasn't keen to repeat, even if I'd felt bad for the dragon after it ate my food and reacted badly.

I'd ended up repressing by an elemental incursion threatening farms and forest, along with an elderly witch, Kath, and her mage husband Ron (not to mention their djinn and the werewolves). To be honest, it hadn't been anything like what I'd expected, and I had been very happy to continue on my bus journey in pursuit of a less physical adventure.

On the last leg of that journey, Kath had asked me to take over their magical bookshop. It turned out that she and Ron were ready to retire, and had no-one to turn over the business to. Of *course* I leapt at the opportunity. I wasn't sure what they would have done if I hadn't crossed their path, but it was the sort of chance I hadn't even dreamed was possible. Kath had seen me to the door of the bookshop last night and handed over the key, before heading off to catch her cruise with Ron. I was almost certain she'd left her grimoire in the bookshop too, but I'd worry about that later.

Talk about a big day! I was still buzzing from the unexpected stroke of fortune. And dithering. I'd never worked in retail, and I didn't really know what I was doing—but I was sure I could learn. After all, I'd learned everything barring the actual Seeing part of my family's business. And my sister's letter (found on the mat in front of the shop door when I arrived last night) had suggested I'd succeed in this business. However much I resented Seers in general and my family in particular just now, a small part of me was reassured by the suggestion that all would be well.

Closing the door and descending the stairs from the apartment into the shop, I paused halfway to survey my new domain. There was certainly plenty of stock. There was also a layer of dust over most of the books, although strangely, not along the tops of the shelves. Descending the rest of the stairs, I ran a finger along the top of one shelf and examined the clean tip. Odd. Still, my stomach was sending me hunger vibes. I wasn't in the mood for a mystery.

I'd found it hard to find my way among the shelves last night. The books weren't ordered in anything like what I'd considered a logical manner. I decided that I wouldn't open today; instead, after breakfast I would organise everything to my liking. That was probably the best way to familiarise myself with what was on hand, too. A smile tugged at my lips at the prospect of diving into what was effectively the biggest library I'd set foot in. It was the first real sense of joy I'd felt since losing Rex, my dog, back on my cousin's farm. I shoved the thought of Rex far, far away. I couldn't deal with those thoughts just now.

My stomach growled again as I prowled the stacked shelves. Right, breakfast first. This was a job worth doing on a full stomach, so I could keep going as long as I needed to. I pulled the front door closed and locked it with the key Kath had given me, then unlocked, and raised the wide-patterned grill which made a sort of airlock area between the door and the outdoors. The grill was secured with a padlock and a short chain which could be reached from either side, thanks to the large holes in the metal that formed it. I flicked the grill with a fingernail as I pulled it down to close up the shop. It was iron, but cunningly fashioned so that it rolled up. Probably someone had been thinking about keeping away the fairies when it was made.

The noodle shop on one side of the bookshop was closed now; hardly surprising, it had had long queues late into the night. The second-hand shop was also closed, but I wasn't so flustered as I'd been on arrival yesterday: I noted that some of the clothes it had on display in the front window were probably worth a look later. I couldn't remember the last time I shopped for clothes in person. Living rurally, I usually ordered something online and hoped that it would fit—or, if I wanted assurance, I asked my younger sister Delphine to foresee the fit. Maybe there *were* some upsides to a Seer lifestyle that I hadn't considered when I left home. Leaving the closed shops behind me, I crossed the road to see what I could find to eat.

The road was bisected by a flower garden, bright blooms distracting from the grimy asphalt. Further along, a trio of palm trees ruffled their fronds in the middle of a roundabout; looking past them I could catch glimpses of the inner harbour. Near the intersection was a hole-in-the-wall coffee shop that appealed for its tiny simplicity, but it only sold biscotti from a jar; not what I had in mind as book-sorting fuel. I passed a couple more closed restaurants—I could hardly believe how many were concentrated in such a small area; city people must eat out a lot more than I considered normal—before I found what I was looking for by following my nose through the door: a bakery.

Inside, fancy cakes were arrayed behind glass. Baguettes and sourdough competed for space behind the counter. Packets of biscuits and brownies crowded a shelf to one side. Although it was still early, I had to queue to make my order. Popularity was definitely a good sign. I pondered what to pick while I waited my turn. Should I get one of the cheese and basil croissants? Or a healthy but rather pretentious brie baguette? Or what about a cheese pretzel? There were several hanging on a wooden stick on the wall beside the sourdough.

In the end I opted for a takeaway cup of green tea for the novelty value, the cheese and basil croissant, which was huge and golden, promising buttery goodness, as well as a cherry-and-whipped-cream filled choux pastry that I promised myself I'd wait to eat until *after* I'd been through at least half of the books in the bookshop. Well, maybe a third. Definitely a quarter.

Juggling my purchases and wishing I'd thought to pack a shopping bag, I almost threw my tea in the face of a customer who came through the doorway as I tried to go out.

"Sorry, are you alright?" I gasped, as hot green tea spattered the newcomer's T-shirt.

"Fine," he said gruffly, in a voice that seemed oddly familiar.

My gaze travelled up, but not very far; the gold-flecked, hazel eyes that met mine belonged to the somewhat short, blond-ringleted werewolf who'd travelled on the bus with me yesterday.

"Oh, er... good?" I said, wishing my voice didn't sound so uncertain. Of *course* it was a good thing he was OK. I just hadn't expected to see a familiar face in this city. Especially not a familiar face with long canines. Even if he wasn't snarling, they were rather intimidating. Plus, werewolves were predators. Everyone I'd grown up with had been full of stories about the violent nature of werewolves.

The predatory, fanged man stepped aside so I could exit, patting my shoulder on his way into the bakery in a brotherly way that was somehow disappointing.

"Order ready?" he asked the baker, who I could see behind the counter, assembling several paper bags full of baked goods.

"Here you go, Dirk. Hope the pack likes the new flavour of buns; I put a few caraway seeds in this lot." The baker chatted amiably away about the food he'd prepared. "It's going on the account as usual, right?" he added as he handed the bags over.

"Yes."

Well, at least it wasn't just me missing out on a full conversation from the werewolf.

Another person approached me from the street. "Excuse me, please." Red-haired and with a bitter twist to her lips, the new customer was clearly displeased at my presence.

"Oh. sorry." Realising I'd been blocking the doorway, I turned away from the bakery. Werewolf or no, it was time to get to work. I had a job to do.

Chapter Two

I'd finished the dregs of the green tea and most of the croissant before I re-entered the bookshop. I wasn't sure if I liked the green tea; it was more bitter than I'd expected. But the croissant was quite possibly the best thing I'd ever eaten. If this was city life, bring it on.

Opening the door to the bookshop, I noticed an odd mustiness that I was certain hadn't been there before. And was that smoke wafting along the floor? Anxiety clenched my stomach. Surely there was nothing to spark a fire in here. I scoffed the last bite of croissant and licked my buttery fingers. Whatever was going wrong, greasy fingerprints on the books wouldn't help.

Following the smoke between the aisles, a rising sense of dread made my quick footsteps feel slow. I rounded the end of the first bookshelf. There was nothing untoward there, but I thought I heard something scratching in the ceiling. Still, scratching wasn't fire; I probably just needed to lay some mousetraps. I kept going down the next aisle, smoke wafting with every step. Was it really smoke though? There was no burning smell, and certainly nothing making my eyes water like the smoke in the forest yesterday. I narrowed my unwatering eyes. The smoke wasn't purple like Ron's djinn had been. But it wasn't quite as mundane as it was trying to appear either. I turned around the final stack and arrived at the velvet curtain which disguised the scrolls and the more expensive grimoires. *There.*

Smoke poured out from beneath the curtain. I whipped it aside, and sure enough, a grimoire whose cover I was sure I recognised, decorated as it was with an intricate pattern that could be Celtic, or then again might be locally inspired, was open on the floor, flipping its pages to and fro. Smoke billowed from the book, wafted aloft by the flipping pages.

"What are you doing?" I demanded, feeling rather silly as I spoke aloud to a book. At least it wasn't an inanimate object, I consoled myself. The pages stopped flipping, and the book fell open invitingly. Clearly, I was supposed to read this page. "All right, what's the problem?" I bent down to read, waving smoke away from my face. "Can you stop with the smoke? It's hard enough to see in here as it is, with no windows for natural light." Squinting a little, I read.

Paw prints in the dust below,
Intruders indicated above.
Though ever alone I go,
Togetherness I would love.

I suppressed a groan. The grimoire's poetry hadn't been improved by its journey, clearly. But I remembered Kath's warning—don't insult the grimoire—and didn't speak my thoughts aloud. Instead, I tried to puzzle out the meaning of the rhyme.

I *had* noticed scuffs in the dust. The mousetraps had better be a priority.

"OK, I'll deal with the mice. But... you're a book."

The pages flipped warningly before opening again on the same poem. There was another line below it now, clearly separate thanks to the white space around it.

Identification is the first step to success.

"Alright, a grimoire, not just a book." I amended my description. "I..." I decided that telling the grimoire it was supposed to be alone wasn't a winning strategy. "Would you like to be put up behind the cash register so you can see what's going on?" That should be just as safe a spot as hidden away in the alcove. But there was more page-flipping. I wished it would just write another poem; hard though the poems were to interpret, page-flips weren't very clear, either. "Right, so you don't want to be on display?"

One page turned emphatically.

"I'll take that as a no. So what do you want? There are plenty of other books around you." I looked behind me at the rows and rows of books. "Did you want to be placed with some different books?" There was a gust of wind and the magical smoke swirled high. I coughed. It might not make my eyes water, but it had enough substance to impede my breathing. The grimoire's pages flipped excitedly. "Looks like that's a yes. But so far, I don't know what other books there are, so if you can clear up this smoke, I can get on with cataloguing everything. Then I'll know what else there is, and maybe where to shelve you. All right?"

A single page flipped over.

"I'm assuming that means yes." I hesitated. One page flip had meant no before. It wasn't a great mode of communication, but I felt sure the grimoire would let me know if I got things wrong. "No more smoke, OK? I'll work as fast as I can."

The grimoire was still, and I thought that perhaps the smoke slowed a little. That was probably as close to agreement as I was going to get. Now I'd just have to find some windows to clear the smoke so I could see to start sorting books.

Chapter Three

THE LEPRECHAUN

There were no windows to open downstairs.

I'd scoured the front, back and side walls of the bookshop, and all I'd come up with was the front door and the stairs to my apartment.

After some thought, I opened every window in the apartment upstairs, pausing to appreciate the bathroom view of the shield volcano in the harbour when I did so.

I left my cream-filled choux pastry on the kitchen bench, then headed downstairs to open the front door. I made sure the 'closed' sign was still showing clearly, and made a start on sorting through the books near the door. Before long, the smoke had begun to clear, sucked out through the upstairs windows by the draught I'd created with my strategic openings. I settled myself on a small footstool I found under the counter, and started looking through the bookshelves, which—apart from the book-lined walls—weren't aligned in any obvious way, but instead angled this way and that.

I was entranced by the range of subjects on display—and slightly horrified at the lack of organisation. 'Macro diets for mermaids'—a cookbook leaning heavily on raw fish and seaweed, I discovered when I curiously flipped through it—was wedged in between a treatise on dwarven economic policies and a primer of nymph biology. How did customers ever find what they wanted? It was a good thing I'd decided not to open today. I made piles of books by subject, and vowed to invest in a laptop as soon as I could. I'd used an aged desktop at home to run statistical models, which obviously hadn't been practical to take with me on the bus. Not to mention I'd had no desire to run financial futures models in whatever my new life turned out to be. Still, it was a puzzle to me. How had Kath and Ron controlled their stock?

At least each book had a price scrawled in pencil on the inside cover, so I wouldn't have to make those up out of thin air. I lost track of time as I sorted and made piles of books with similar themes. I reached the end of one stack and moved around to the other side. The books were similarly disorganised on that side. I had created a lot of piles by the time a noise at the door startled me out of my focus.

'Would you be thinking of opening today?' A thready voice with a hint of an accent made its way inside along with a ray of sunlight that made the book it landed on appear gold rather than simply yellow.

Still seated, now by a pile of books about mage hierarchies, I tracked the voice back to its source. A leprechaun, possibly one of the ones from the bus yesterday, stood in the doorway, looking hopeful.

'Sorry, but no.' I waved a hand at the chaos around me. 'I've a lot more to get organised before I can think of opening.'

'Tomorrow, perchance?' He raised his bushy eyebrows hopefully at me.

I raised my eyebrows right back; I hadn't heard anyone use the word 'perchance' outside of a book. Then I realised I was being rude to a potential customer and cast a look around the shop. I had a *lot* more books to get through.

'It seems unlikely.'

He continued to stare at me, widening his eyes. His mouth turned down at the corners and his eyebrows raised towards the centre of his forehead. Was that a hint of entreaty?

'What were you looking for?' I asked.

The leprechaun squared his shoulders—which were about level with my head where I sat on the floor—and clasped his hands behind his back before proclaiming:

> *'Why, it's instructions I need*
> *Though I cannot read*
> *If gold is here to be found*
> *It is not in the ground.'*

I let my forehead sink onto the wooden edge of the shelf in front of me. It clunked satisfyingly. Of *course* the leprechaun was after gold. But...

'Really can't read? Why come to a bookshop then?'

'I must make the rhyme
If I have the time
At maps I can look
And use audiobooks.'

He gave me a triumphant smile, presumably pleased he'd managed to rhyme his answer. Admittedly, he had done it better than I would have been able to. I had no idea yet if the shop contained either maps or audiobooks, but I shouldn't put off a customer if I was going into business. And it seemed that I was.

'Er... Friday?' I'll put up a sign. Um, and the door will be open,' I added hastily. I wasn't sure how serious he was about not being able to read.

'Bright and pleasant
morning to you.

Though rodents may
descend anew
At least you'll know
there's not a shrew.'

I stared at the little man, slightly aghast. Was there no end to prophesying? I'd thought I'd got away from that by coming to the city, and here was someone trying to provide foreknowledge on my very first day. The leprechaun frowned at me, clearly expecting a response.

'Er, thanks,' I said. 'Um, good to know about the shrew.' That alone made his rhyme suspect; we didn't have shrews in our country. Just assorted introduced rats and mice.

He nodded and turned away.

Great. If the leprechaun was to be believed, the incident with the grimoire wasn't the end of my difficulties this morning. And I'd given myself a deadline for opening too. Still, that was probably for the best. I got to my feet, dusting off my knees. It was time to try that cream-filled pastry. Surely I was a quarter of the way through the books by now? I closed and locked the door to prevent random intruders and made my way along a different aisle, checking book titles as I went. Hopefully I'd be able to get through every book by my self-imposed deadline, but if not, every bit of information I could glean about the stock would help. My eyes passed over 'Naiads: a primer for dummies' (something I might look at later—I'd never seen a naiad in the flesh), stacked right next to 'Blood'n'Bone'.

At first I thought that was a gardening manual, but on closer inspection I saw the subtitle was 'How to feed your zombie'. Much less wholesome. I wrinkled my nose. I didn't want to encourage *anyone* to feed zombies. Maybe I should quietly remove that book. Beside it was 'Up! A career speedwitch's story', which seemed to be an autobiography. A higher shelf held a selection of cookbooks which appeared completely mundane, apart from the pictures on their covers. 'Macro' displayed a blue whale and a kraken arrayed on a plate. That one was definitely coming off the shelves; no way was I selling a cookbook which included endangered species. 'Soda bread and farls' looked like something that would appeal to my leprechaun visitor, and to mundanes too. But 'A Compendium of Faerie' would have to be reshelved, unless it was a far darker tome than I anticipated.

Later, I promised myself. *I'll get to all the books later.* Right now, I had a cream puff waiting with my name on it. I set off up the stairs with a will.

Chapter Four

THE RODENTS

Opening the door that led to my new over-bookshop flat, a scuttling noise from the direction of the kitchen drew a surprised gasp from me. I hurried the few steps to that room, but stopped in the doorway, covering my mouth with a hand in horror. My long-awaited cherry cream choux pastry was all but gone. Only a gnawed crust and a streak of cream and cherry jam remained on the plate. I felt hollow with more than hunger.

The leprechaun's rodent comments had been far too prophetic—unless birds had somehow invaded through the windows I'd left open? I peered around the small flat, but no birds flapped anywhere. Besides, the leprechaun had suggested rodents. Maybe I needed to invest in more than a few mousetraps. I edged closer to the empty plate, mourning the loss of my snack, but not wanting to step on anything small and furry either.

Sure enough, jammy footprints led a merry dance across my formerly clean bench. I counted. Unless the culprit had danced a jig on the plate and bench, there'd been more than one rodent. I measured the prints with my fingers, wishing for a ruler I didn't have. I'd have to see if I could find an identification guide downstairs, but based on my experience of mice back home, these were either mice of unusual size, or not mice at all. I set my teeth and resolved to find a rat trap as well as an identification guide. No way was I having rats stealing my food or dancing on my kitchen bench. But where were they now?

I examined the bench closely. At some point, the rats must have stopped and cleaned themselves, because the helpful prints stopped just shy of the edge of the bench. Crossing my arms grumpily, I stood back to examine the kitchen. Where could rats have hidden in a tiny kitchen like this one? There was a range hood venting the oven, but fine mesh covered the tube leading to the outdoors. Sandwiched between the stairs and the lounge, and backing onto the building next door, the kitchen didn't have any windows. Only electric lights and pale yellow walls enlivened the room.

Uncrossing my arms again, I bent over to check underneath the cupboards. *There.* At the end of the row of cupboard doors was a narrow gap. Caught on the wood on one side was a smudge of cream and a few pale ginger hairs. I frowned at them. I'd never heard of a ginger rat. Still, no matter what colour it was, I didn't want it in my kitchen.

"Fair warning," I said aloud. "I'll be buying traps this afternoon. And making wards too. And you'd better hope that bakery has more cherry cream choux pastries, because I was looking *forward* to that. There will be *no* rats in my kitchen. This is your chance to get out, and stay out."

I felt slightly silly speaking to invisible rats, but after all, Mum had once told us about the time she'd had an encounter with harvest mice who repaired dolls' clothes. On the whole, it seemed like a good idea to give the rats a chance to run away. Besides, speaking to unseen rodents wasn't much different than talking to books.

I wanted a cup of tea to keep me going, but I also felt that I'd need to do a thorough disinfect of the kitchen before it would be safe to eat in again, so I decided to go out once more. My bank balance wouldn't thank me for eating out so much, but it was probably just as well to explore the area now. I'd be busy in retail hours once I opened the shop for real.

Sadly, the bakery was closed. I must have worked on the books for longer than I'd realised. I cast a longing glance through its windows, but there wasn't even a bread roll in sight. I gave up on the bakery for the day and went in search of the mall. Following a wide footpath paved in alternating grey and pink tiles, I rounded the corner, ascended a slight hill, and located the entrance to the mall without difficulty. Inside, there was a supermarket that furnished me with some basic rat traps and a jumbo bottle of bleach. I added a packet of green tea bags and on impulse, put a jar of chocolate powder in my trolley. Life couldn't be all green tea. I also rummaged through the herb and stationery aisles for some basic warding materials. Usually I'd make wards from what I had available, but I hadn't thought to bring more than a few crystals in my backpack. Visionary dreams and a brave heart (the sorts of things crystals were advised for) wouldn't stop a rat invasion. Actually, the average rat was smart enough to out-think a ward, too, but a well-placed rune could at least help lead them to the rat traps. A lifetime of training to be a Seer had introduced me to a broad range of magical assists.

A pack of pita bread, eggs, some feta and a can of beans completed my shop, though they added to my meal repertoire rather than to my wards or cleaning supplies. Since I had got lucky with accommodation, my savings would last longer than I'd planned, but that didn't mean I was going to spend up big on food before I was earning. Then again... I extricated myself from the checkout queue long enough to add some basic baking supplies and a bottle of cream. I considered the pile of food in my trolley, then turned back to the vegetable section to find some salad ingredients. Mum would never forgive me if I didn't include salad in my diet, no matter how good the bakery was. And it wasn't as if Dad's garden was here to provide such things. Once the kitchen was clean and warded, I could save money by making my own sweet treats. Even if they weren't up to the standard of the bakery on the corner. I promised myself I'd visit the bakery again during its opening hours, as a private celebration when I completed my stocktake of the bookshop. If it was frequented by a certain werewolf... I'd have to hope that his predatory urges were satisfied by bakery food.

I was worried about having a werewolf pack nearby, but I told myself, firmly, that it was all part of moving to the city. No doubt there'd be all sorts of people that I'd never met before. And that was probably a *good* thing. Definitely. Better than having my every move predicted, at any rate.

I strode out of the mall with my head held high and my arms dragged low by the weight of my shopping bags. A bubble of pure joy rose up at the idea that I could be any sort of person I wanted, in the anonymity of a big city.

Chapter Five

The feeling lasted as far as the door of the bookshop. While I was wrestling with the padlock and chain combination that secured the grill, my shopping bags at my feet, a couple of teenagers approached me. One was dressed from head to toe in black: black dress, black lace gloves, black boots, and a black scarf on their head. Their obviously fake lashes fluttered in the brisk breeze that had started blowing as I walked back down the hill, admiring the view of the harbour and hoping that the volcano out there was dormant.

The other teen wore jeans and a T-shirt, but had round blue earrings with an inset silver witch-on-a-broomstick in each ear. Both of them had long flowing locks. It looked like the inevitable teenage witch crowd had found me. Well, good. If they were anything like my younger sister Delphine, they'd be good customers, within the limits of their budgets. All through her teen years, Delphine had spent most of her weekly allowance on fortune-telling aids. Of course, they worked—for her.

"Are you going to be open soon?" the black-clad one asked. "Because I've been waiting for a tarot guide for*ever*, and I kind of need it now."

"I'll open on Friday," I told her, or possibly them. The witch had an androgynous look which made me doubt my first impression of femininity.

"Can't you sell me one now? I need to do a reading for a friend. And it's kind of hard to do without a guide." They bounced on the balls of their black-shod feet, indicating urgency.

"I'm sorry, I haven't had a chance to sort out the stock yet. I haven't found tarot guides yet, but given what I've seen so far, there definitely will be something like that," I assured them. I didn't want to lose a potential customer, but there was no way I was ready to start selling things today.

"Couldn't you look now?"

"Really, that wouldn't do any good. It will take me until Friday *at least* to get the shop in order. Have you used tarot cards before now?" I looked the teen in the eye. "Because even with a guide there's a lot of interpretation involved. I'd suggest you start with a straightforward pendulum, if your reading is urgent." Looking back at my shopping bags, I noticed a line of ants heading towards them from the direction of the grill. I was absolutely not ready to share my groceries with ants. I picked up the bags and moved them away from the insects, awkwardly clutching their handles with the keys still in my hand.

Both teens still hovered.

"Are you going to be getting crystal balls in? Because the last people here wouldn't, but I'd totally buy one if you did," the girl with the witchy earrings said in a rush of words. Her hands clutched each other, twisting nervously.

I jiggled the key in the padlock. It was a tricky fit; I didn't remember Kath having any difficulty with it last night. And it had closed without difficulty—of course, padlocks always did. The key still wouldn't go in, so I addressed the teen's questions. At least crystal balls were something I felt I had some experience with, unlike running a retail business.

"I'll look into it," I promised. "I'll have to find out what the supply chains are like here though. I've just arrived." I turned to the teen in black. "I'm sure there are some tarot guides in the bookshop somewhere. Do you already have a tarot deck, or are you looking for one of those too?"

They looked into the middle distance for a moment, possibly trying to cultivate an air of mystery—or then again, perhaps trying to stop those long lashes from coming loose in the wind, which was getting fiercer with every passing moment.

"I've got a second-hand deck," they said, facing towards me again and shading their eyes with a hand. "But if you have others, I could be interested." They looked away again. Definitely trying to maintain an aura of mystery, I decided, but also struggling with the wind-lash combination. Still, I didn't want to shame a potential customer, so I pretended not to notice.

"I'll keep an eye out for tarot decks while I'm doing my stocktake," I told them. "If I can't find any, I'll order some in."

"Thanks," both teens chorussed, then sauntered away in the direction of the bus stop.

At this rate, Friday might be a busy opening day—so long as I could get back into the shop before then. I jiggled the key again, then pulled it out of the padlock to inspect it. There was some sort of blue goo on it, a bit like chewing gum, but with a more granular consistency. Had someone meddled with my padlock? I tilted the padlock up so I could look into it. I had to push my hair out of my face to see properly; it had come loose from the bobby pins that held it back while I talked to the teens. Sure enough, the same blue stuff filled the padlock. I doubted the teens were the source. They hadn't been by the door when I arrived. Looking closely at it, I decided it was probably the excretion of some sort of insect. Maybe the ants had been stuffing weird ant-food into it. I looked down at the line of ants, more closely this time. Sure enough, it stretched up the side of the wall beside the grill, and some of the ants were carrying blue granules. I'd have to add insect repellent to my wards in future.

I gritted my teeth in frustration. I didn't have anything in my shopping bags to deal with random goo. Another lock of hair fell forward, and I impatiently brushed it back again. Halfway through the action, I stopped, feeling the bobby pin stuck halfway down the lock of my hair. My gritted teeth turned into a grin of triumph as I pulled the pin out.

"Hair furniture to the rescue," I said aloud as I used the bobby pin to scrape blue goo out of the padlock. Delphine had always said bobby pins were the most multipurpose form of hair accessory, and it seemed that she was right. I'd worry about adding insect repellants to the bookshop door later. Once I'd found a book on insect wards.

Chapter Six

THE GROWLING

At first, I thought it was my stomach growling at me when I got inside. It was well past lunchtime, after all.

But my stomach had never sounded quite so... visceral, even on those occasions when I'd ignored bodily requirements in favour of an all-day deep dive into some mathematical way of predicting the future, like modelling marriage and divorce rates after severe storms.

This growling was the sort that set my arm hair on end and made me wonder if I should have learnt self-defence before jumping on a bus to the city. And it was coming from near the back of the bookshop.

My feet planted themselves beside the cookery books near the door and refused to move. I was inclined to agree with my feet on this occasion, but the stairs to my apartment were in that direction too. I'd locked my apartment door as a matter of course when I left, but that meant that I couldn't make a dash for my room without having to pause for a significant amount of time on the way. As I hesitated, the sound morphed into an otherworldly howl which echoed around the bookshop (how did it manage to echo in a space with so many books for insulation, my errant brain wondered?) then died down into something closer to a sob. I felt better about dealing with sobs. They implied some sort of fear or remorse, surely?

"Who's there?" I asked loudly. "Can I help?"

The sobs paused briefly, as though considering, then resumed. Well. Now what? I supposed there was nothing for it but to plunge into the bookshop and see who or what was back there. After all, if I was going to run the bookshop, I couldn't have random growls emerging from the depths. It would scare off customers.

I set down my shopping and took a tentative step forward, then another. I grabbed the copy of Blood'n'Bone as I went past it. It had a good heft to it, which might prove useful. Thus armed, I strode a few steps. I was brought up short by the sight of the grimoires and scrolls alcove bathed in dark blue light. The light was pulsating in time with the intermittent sobs. Holding up Blood'n'Bone like a shield, I advanced cautiously. The sobbing seemed to be coming from the alcove too. Close enough to see at last—much helped by the blue glow—I couldn't see anything wrong at first. But as my eyes adjusted, I realised that the carved grimoire that Kath had left was lying on the floor of the alcove. The glow was coming from its pages. And so were the sobs.

I dropped to my knees beside the grimoire. "All right then," I muttered. "What seems to be the problem?"

The sobs transmuted into an occasional hiccup, and the book flipped its pages over. I bent over to read the page when it stopped flipping, clutching the zombie feeding guide to my chest. The text wandered across the page as though written there by a whimsical hand.

I wandered lonely as a cloud
With not a single daffodil in sight
Alone, all all alone,
I waited for the gath'ring night.

Huh. It seemed that like me, the grimoire had been exposed to Wordsworth at some time in its past.

"So, you're still lonely. You know, it's only been a couple of hours. I haven't exactly had time to find you a friend," I told it.

The grimoire riffled its pages again.

This time the text was densely packed and formal, in a typewritten font. I squinted to read it in the dimness of the bookshop interior. The light from the grimoire was noticeably fainter now it had my attention.

Why didn't they have windows back here? Surely a little sun damage would have been more than made up for by not having to switch on a light every time the store was open? It couldn't be healthy to rely on a grimoire glowing for you, either. I read.

Hamsters make wonderful pets when properly socialized. They will need a large habitat to ensure natural behaviour. The optimum diet for your newly acquired hamster is one that is as close as possible to what they would eat in the wild.

I rocked back on my heels.

"No way," I said. "I am not housing *hamsters* for you. Besides, they don't even live in this country. We've got three types of rats, mice, *and* guinea pigs in the rodent line. I'm not sure if rabbits and chinchillas count. But we don't need anything else."

The grimoire closed with a snap, and thick smoke started exuding from its closed pages.

"I'm sorry you're lonely," I said. "And I've told you I'll do what I can. Just give me a chance, OK?" Feeling somewhat foolish—what might the grimoire do with the information, after all?—I placed Blood'n'Bone on the floor besidebeside the grimoire. I hesitated a moment, then opened it to the first page. Who knew if a sentient grimoire could turn the pages of a book? But it had to be worth a try. "Here's some unusual reading for you. It might pass the time. Alright?"

The smoke curled back on itself, sucked back into the grimoire. The blue glow shaded into lilac, and the sobbing stopped echoing in my ears.

"Let me know if you need another book before bedtime," I told the grimoire. I didn't hear any further noises, but as I watched, a puff of wind that seemed to come from nowhere flipped the first page of Blood'n'Bone over to the second. *Well, that seems to be going alright.*

I backed away towards the front door where I'd left my grocery bags, and locking the front door, I grabbed the lot and raced upstairs. The skittering sound as I opened the door to my apartment was probably just my imagination.

Chapter Seven

THE APARTMENT

I decided not to risk going downstairs again for a while. Instead, I unpacked my groceries, taking pleasure in finding homes for everything. It was so different from living at home, where everything already had its place. Kath and Ron couldn't have lived in the apartment for a long time, because every cupboard was empty, at least of food. There were a couple of plates, a bowl, and a mug. In the old-fashioned pull-out warming drawer under the oven I found a rusty metal casserole dish. It looked like I'd be visiting the secondhand shop as soon as it opened, for more than just clothes. I liked to bake, and I would definitely need more than just a casserole. Meanwhile, I mixed up a batch of brownies in the bowl, melting chocolate and butter before I added eggs and flour. I set them to bake in the casserole dish, then spent a happy half hour puttering around my new abode, deciding where to set up wards: on the windowsills and over the door frame where the stairs led down to the shop.

I discovered the best view was from the bathroom, which faced away from the street. The back sides of other shops and apartments stretched out to the right and left, with occasional gaps for driveways. There was native bush far below, as the hill dropped away sharply behind the shops—apparently too steep to have been denuded for houses. Although I'd wanted to move to a city, I found myself unexpectedly comforted by the presence of bush so close by. If my dad were here, he'd no doubt find a path to the trees, in order to listen to what they had to say. That was his primary method of forecasting, after all. I couldn't hear the leaves whispering to each other, except in the mundane way they moved in the wind. But it was pleasant to have them there.

If I looked across the hillside, my view encompassing another suburb or three, I could see the shield volcano that dominated the harbour standing tall on the horizon. At that moment it had a backdrop of blue sky and scattered clouds, and looked serene. I resolved to find a book on the geology of the area. Serenity was a wonderful state for a volcano, but was it likely to stay that way? If I was going to live here for any length of time, I wanted to know. Besides, my Seer's training was heavily ingrained. Volcanoes could affect financial futures, so geology was relevant.

Apart from the bathroom, the bedroom, and the kitchen, the only other room (besides the hall connecting everything) was a living-dining area. It already held a couch and a desk. There wasn't space for a lot else. But coming from having only a room to call my own, it seemed positively palatial.

The timer for the brownies went off, and I retrieved the treat, setting it on top of the stove to cool off while I put together some simple wards for my windowsills.

I shouldn't need anything fancy. What would try to get into a bookshop, after all?

I assembled salt from the supermarket, a pinch of stinky rue from the stash I'd brought with me, a sprig of rather better-smelling rosemary from the street plantings I'd passed on the way home, and a few crystals (clear quartz, amethyst and citrine, also from my bag) to place on each warding site. If nothing else, the wards might slow down mosquitos.

Warding sites are usually dictated by points of access: doorways and windows were the usual ones. I placed one ward in the bathroom, using the clear quartz. Another went in the living room (citrine there), and one over the door which led down to the bookshop. I put one of each crystal there, since it was the most likely to come into contact with intruders. Finally, I put a ward with an amethyst in the bedroom window, which looked out over the street. There was a street tree out there too, clothed in yellow blossoms. It took away some of the heat from the asphalted road and the tiled street. While I was placing wards and crystals, a bus drew up not far down the street. A tall figure wearing a cloak, hat and sunglasses descended from the bus and walked in the direction of my shop. Was it yet another would-be customer? I'd have to get the shop opened as soon as I could, if there was so much passing trade even while it was closed.

Sure enough, there was a rapping sound as the figure knocked on the shop grill downstairs and rattled the padlock. I peered out of the window, careful not to disturb my newly positioned wards. I didn't want to risk the grimoire's ire again just yet, and I definitely wasn't ready to open the shop.

The figure appeared to be writing something on a small pad, although the street tree's blossom-laden branches obscured my view somewhat. After a short time, the person bent, and presumably pushed a piece of paper under the grill, then swirled their cloak around them dramatically. It looked as though a cloud of darkness surrounded them for a moment. When it dissipated, a small bat hovered where the figure had stood, wings flapping frantically. Then with a series of jerky swoops, it fluttered away.

I sank down onto the bed, which was conveniently close to the window. Although now I came to think of it, perhaps it was *too* close. I didn't want my bed to be visible to vampires. I shuddered. Vamps were worse than werewolves, if my family were right. And annoyingly, they usually were.

"Phew," I said aloud, feeling the need to voice my thoughts even though there was no-one around to tell. "Who knew this shop would be frequented by vampires? Let alone bats." Although I supposed I should be pleased that there were bats around; I was certain that I'd seen something about the rarity of bats. Did vampiric bats count?

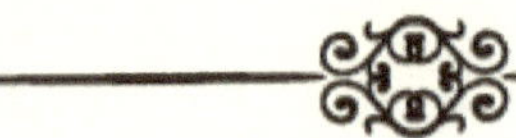

After I'd finished placing my wards and the few things I'd brought with me, and eaten more pieces of brownie than was strictly necessary, I headed back down to the bookshop. I had a lot more books to sort, and they weren't going to order themselves. I had a brief vision of books flying through the air in some sort of orderly waltz, re-stacking themselves appropriately. I snorted softly at the thought. That was wizards work, and even they employed librarians. Besides, even if I *could* have magically sorted the books, I wouldn't know what was in them myself without actually looking. I had to remind myself several times over the next few hours that knowing one's stock was a good thing. I added a fourth skull-emblazoned dictionary of the dead to my stack. I wasn't sure who would want such a thing; perhaps that was why there were so many. If no-one bought them, perhaps they multiplied in dark corners. The next book was conceivably related, since it listed types of stone and their associated fae or kobolds. I decided that it should probably be shelved in non-fiction along with the other books on mythological creatures, and turned to the next book, then the next, and the next.

Chapter Eight

FLAMINGOS AND GREMLINS

Later, I retrieved the paper from the front door—the grimoire had let a few whimpers keen through the shop, but didn't repeat its earlier antics—and found it was a polite request for opening hours. It was just a shame that the words appeared to be scrawled in blood.

Maybe it's just red ink. Yeah, right. Because vampires always write in red ink. I wasn't convincing myself at all well. I just hoped there wasn't more than one vampire in the area. Vampires were territorial, like werewolves, I thought.

Putting aside my concerns, I carefully wrote out a sign for the shop door on a piece of paper I'd found in the desk drawer, promising a Friday opening. That left me with two days to get everything sorted out. I looked into ordering some additional signs to promote the opening, and decided it was too complicated. I'd have to stick with my hand-written sign.

Then I spent some time examining the till. Once I'd figured out that a single button opened it, I realised I'd better have a go at operating it for real. Instead of the compartments I vaguely expected to find for coins and cash, it opened onto a black void that seemed to swallow light. I bit my lip and shoved the cash drawer closed again, and ran upstairs to grab my wallet. This time, I tried pressing some numbers on the till: $18.99—an imaginary transaction for an imaginary book sale.

Then I pressed the button to open the cash drawer. A purple glow emanated from deep inside it this time. Hesitantly, I put in a twenty-dollar note. The note was sucked out of my hand into the glow, and a couple of coins were somehow spat out, coming to a standstill just outside the glowing area as though in a perfectly normal register. Apparently, this cash register calculated change. A smile broke out on my face. I didn't mind maths, but a self-regulating cash register was going to save me a lot of work. Then I remembered that Kath had mentioned that customers might pay in more than just cash. I didn't want to risk placing jewellery in the register, but I did have a couple more crystals. I retrieved one and tried another transaction. The purple glow pulsed sullenly. Had I not given enough value? Or...

"I'd like change in coins," I said experimentally. Nothing happened. Nervously, I pushed my hand into the purple glow, thinking to get my crystal back, at least. An odd tugging sensation pulled at my hand, and I let it drift right. My fingers were moved up and down—a waggle, I decided to call it—and I felt the distinctive cool metal discs of coins. "Thank you!" I exclaimed. Encouraged by my success, I decided I could risk a necklace.

Further experimentation gave me the idea that the cash register had built-in pocket universes for coin exchange. I discovered I could get the currency and/or item of value I wanted by sticking my hand into the glow and giving it a twist. Three twists for gold, four for jewels, and the weird finger waggle for dollars and cents. I had no idea if it would work for regular electronic transactions, so I set up my phone to deal with those. It took all my skill and education to work out that part. I wondered how other people managed without going mad in the process. Perhaps they did. Or they got swallowed by the obscurities of the banking system, or just opted for cash. After that experience, sorting books was positively a joy.

The grimoire seemed to be lonely. It periodically wafted smoke in my direction; nothing like the billowing clouds it had used earlier, but enough to get my attention. The third time I started coughing (while reshelving an encyclopaedia of newts and allied ingredients, a disturbing title at best), I took the book with me.

"If I read a little, will you lay off the smoke?"

The grimoire flipped a page, but no poem appeared.

"I'm going to take that as a yes," I told it. After that, every time I moved to catalogue a new bookshelf, I read aloud a chapter of a random book, seated on the floor beside the grimoire. It was quite an education, but it did add significantly to the time it took to get through the shelves.

In between stocktaking, reorganisation, and reading aloud to the grimoire to stop it smoking me out or howling at me, my brain was scrambling, trying to make sure I had everything organised and ready for opening day. Perhaps it was no surprise that my sleep was disturbed by the sound of pattering in the roof and floor. There was so much to process that my mind generated problems even while I slept. I spent the next couple of days burning the candle at both ends. Small wonder that when I did sleep, my dreams were running around like hamsters on wheels.

I awoke on Thursday morning to the sound of hammering on the shop door. I threw on a light cardigan—that was enough to look like I was dressed, not just wearing an oversized T-shirt, right?—and stumbled downstairs to see a delivery man standing beside a big cardboard box nearly as tall as I was. His van was pulled up across all three of the angled car parks the bookshop shared with the secondhand shop and the noodle house, orange hazard lights blinking.

What now?

"Hello?" I said uncertainly. I was beginning to see the merits of being a Seer—at least, I was experiencing the downsides of *not* being one. My mum would have known exactly what was in the box, and would no doubt have woken early, showered, dressed, and made herself a cup of tea before opening the door a moment before the delivery man knocked. In hindsight, I suspected that she must have enjoyed keeping the local postie off-guard—having the door opened just as you raised your hand to rap on the door must have been very irritating.

Perhaps it's not surprising that our parcels were always being misdelivered back home...

"Delivery for you," the delivery guy said cheerfully, not being subject to premature door-opening.

"I'm not expecting anything that size," I informed him. "How about I check the contents before you race off?"

"You'll need to be quick," he cautioned. "I've another hundred and sixty deliveries to make today. And you'll have to sign for the delivery first. I can't let you open something otherwise."

I shook my head, but he insisted, and in the end I decided it was better to sign and find out what was in the box, than be left forever in the dark. Besides, I wanted to keep the local delivery man onside. I expected I'd need a lot of things delivered to the shop as time went on—more books, at the very least. And tarot cards, crystals, bookmarks... There were a lot of little things I thought might sell, besides books. I tore into the box and pulled out the first item.

By Delphi and Apollo, what is this? I was holding a life-size pink plastic flamingo. There were more in the box. Lots more.

"These aren't mine."

The delivery guy rubbed a hand over his balding head. "Your address is right here," he said. "Is that your name?" He tapped a finger on the delivery slip, which unfortunately did indeed display my name. "You did sign," he reminded me.

"Yes, but I'm sure I didn't order flamingos," I insisted. The only thing I'd ordered was a set of flame-coloured signs to advertise the bookshop. *Flam...* oh, no. I should have known better than to order online. It looked like there were autocorrect gremlins in my phone again. They were a perpetual curse in the futures business. It looked like I'd brought some with me. I gritted my teeth.

"Just put them here," I said, waving vaguely at the space just inside the door. I'd be running an anti-gremlin cycle on my phone just as soon as I'd dealt with the pile of plastic birds that blocked the entrance to the bookshop.

"Sorry, love, I've got to be going. I've spent two minutes extra on this delivery already." The delivery guy was already running back to his van.

Chapter Nine

RODENTS AND GREEN TEA LATTE

I looked over my untouched rat traps with a critical eye: first the ones I'd set up in a few likely spots around the apartment, then at the one hidden in a nook of the bookshop. Sure, rats were smart, but they shouldn't be smart enough to avoid my enspelled traps. Perhaps I needed to change up the bait. Again. I'd already changed it twice. Maybe that was the problem, I was meddling too much. But I wanted results, and fast. It wasn't as bad as if I was running some sort of food shop; at least I didn't have to pass food safety inspections. But I wasn't happy at the prospect of having rats in my abode, especially not when the bookshop opened again. So I kept trying.

I was halfway through swapping out the fragrant blue cheese I'd been using as bait for some spoonfuls of peanut butter laced with cinnamon, which the internet assured me was a superior bait for rats. Or possibly that was a bait meant for possums. Either way, it couldn't perform worse than the cheese. In any case, I was interrupted by a loud squeak, right above my head. I dropped the sticky peanut butter spoon in startlement. Luckily, it landed on bare wooden floorboards, not on a book.

Since it wasn't doing any harm, I ignored the spoon for now, and looked up at the ceiling where it sounded like the squeak had come from. It was probably only in my head that the threatening 'Jaws' signature soundtrack played on a cello, as a ceiling tile was slowly raised by something unseen.

Or, no. It was not in my head.

"Stop that!" I hissed at the grimoire, which had, somehow, flipped tracks on the music player that I'd left playing beside it to keep it company while I was working elsewhere in the shop.

The music switched abruptly to a screeching, intermittent violin. The grimoire was on a roll with the horror film tracks. I took a deep breath, trying to slow my racing heart, and called out in a voice that I'd like to think was strong and unwavering,

"Who's there?"

There was another squeak from the vicinity of the ceiling, and a furry head popped out. The music stopped. That grimoire certainly had a sense of humour. The head didn't belong to a rat. Golden and white fur covered a round face with round ears, and round bulging cheeks. It was a...

"Hamster?" I asked doubtfully. I'd never seen one in the flesh—we don't have them in Aotearoa. Or we didn't. But the cheek pouches seemed distinctive. The music stopped.

The little rodent chittered its teeth and squeaked again. Perhaps that was a yes. It certainly meant that I'd been wrong about the rat infestation. No wonder my traps hadn't worked. Hamsters probably needed seeds or something like that. Perhaps the peanut butter would have worked. But I would have felt terrible about catching a hamster in a rat trap.

"Well, whatever you are, I don't like rodents in the kitchen," I told it. "Keep out of there, all right?"

It squeaked, turned around, displaying a distinct lack of a long rat's tail, and dashed off, letting the ceiling tile drop.

I let out my breath with a puff. "Well," I addressed the grimoire, "I don't know how we got hamsters, but it's a good thing I'm not running a restaurant. I'm sure they wouldn't pass a health inspection. Perhaps they can be company for you?"

The grimoire flipped its pages and music started up again. This time, it was a classical piece. I wasn't all that familiar with classical music, but I thought it was 'Greensleeves'. Not sure if that was a sarcastic comment or agreement, I picked up the peanut-butter-covered spoon and set off to find a damp cloth to mop up the sticky spot on the floor. It seemed I had an infestation of hamsters. Also, my grimoire had unexpected jukebox tendencies. Whatever next?

Late that night, I finished my self-appointed stocktake-and-reorganisation task. Standing at the front door, I surveyed my new domain. I'd dusted shelves (those that weren't already mysteriously free of dust, anyway), sorted books into some sort of logical order, and even set my shoulder to a few bookcases to make more orderly aisles. Now, every shelf gleamed. Displays of attractive books adorned end-shelves, and the velvet curtain disguising the scrolls was adjusted to hang perfectly. The wooden floor didn't really gleam, it didn't have enough varnish for that, but it was as clean as I could make it. A couple of decorative candles stood on either side of the cash register. I was as ready to open the bookshop as I'd ever be.

I woke up early on opening day. Partly it was nerves, but partly it was because of the sound of someone, or something, in the attic. I'd only discovered the attic yesterday, the access hidden inside the one built-in wardrobe that the bedroom possessed. I'd made it to the secondhand shop the day before, and bought a few new clothes suitable for opening a bookshop: linen trousers and a couple of tops that I could mix and match with it. I'd bought another cardigan too. The last couple of evenings had held the promise of autumn, although the calendar told me it was still summer. After my secondhand clothing shop was complete, I'd rummaged around searching for hangers without success—then I looked up. The attic door was more of a square in the ceiling than an actual door, but with the aid of a broomstick and a chair I managed to open it. Peering around with my phone's torch, there had been nothing to see but dust motes and old insulation. Certainly no coat hangers. I'd closed the door again and slid the small locking mechanism shut. My clothes went on a chair beside my bed instead of hanging up.

Now, though, I wondered if I'd disturbed something.

The attic door was locked, but the sound of pacing behind it was unmistakable. I hesitated for a long moment, partly because I was steeling myself to open it, and partly because I was trying to analyse the sound of the footsteps. They didn't belong to anything large. It was more of a scurry than a pace, now I came to analyse the sound. Perhaps the hamsters from the kitchen had retreated to the attic? And what horrors or wonders would the attic of a magical bookshop hold, anyway? Not that I'd found anything particularly magical beyond the grumpy grimoire and the astonishing book selection, so far.

Still, standing outside the door wasn't solving the problem. Research might. I whipped out my phone and started a scholarly search for "footsteps + attic". The results included a range of case studies of elderly aunts, mad wives, banshee habitat plans, and rather a lot of pest control research. None of that was especially reassuring. But it did suggest that I'd have to identify the source of the footsteps if I wanted to do something about them. Also, it seemed likely that ship rats could be the source of the sound. Or possums. Hamsters weren't mentioned, perhaps because they didn't climb, or more likely because they weren't even in the country to *be* a problem.

Retrieving the dining chair (one of a pair of wooden chairs from the living/dining room), I wedged it into the wardrobe again. Fingers trembling slightly, I pulled back the lock and pushed the little square door open with a rush.

Sticking my head up into the attic felt foolish, but it was the only way to see what was there. I came face to face... with a hamster.

"Lords and Ladies, what are you doing here?" I exclaimed in surprise.

"Squeak." The hamster looked at me steadily for a moment, then hightailed it out of sight.

I let out my breath with a whoosh. Apparently I was going to have to learn to live with hamsters *everywhere.*

Downstairs, everything was as I'd left it last night. I'd set up the pink flamingos on either side of the door, figuring that since I'd paid for them, I might as well use them. I'd shied away from online advertising, but the number of people peering in the doorway had increased every day that I'd been sorting books, so I was quietly confident that I'd have at least a few customers. Hopefully all my practising with the cash register meant that I wouldn't make mistakes with it on my first real sale. Assuming I had sales, of course. A brief wave of self-doubt washed over me. How would I know if I'd get sales without a Seer to reassure me of it?

No, I reassured myself. My sister Delphine's note had implied I'd find success, and I had no reason to doubt *her* ability to See, only my own. I decided that what I really needed to start the day off right was a decent bit of food. Something other than the rather stale bread left over from my first supermarket shop.

I checked my phone. Yes, I just had time to nip out for something tasty for breakfast from the corner bakery. It was a good thing it opened before I planned to open the bookshop: there was already a long queue outside the bakery when I arrived. Fortunately the queue moved fast, and before long I was once again hesitating between a cherry choux pastry and something else. Bee Sting slice? Sounded painful, but probably just contained honey. A savoury croissant? An avocado sourdough sandwich? As someone cleared their throat behind me, no doubt impatient for their morning caffeine fix,

I decided I'd need lunch as well. I asked for the sandwich and an opera slice, with a green tea latte. Although I'd decided against buying the plain green tea, the idea of a latte intrigued me. And the opera slice was soaked in coffee as well as being layered with sugary icing, so it would definitely keep me awake. I turned away from the counter clutching my purchases, to find that the werewolf from the other day was the throat-clearer. He didn't look impatient though; instead, he asked me a question.

"Bookshop opening?"

Now that was a question I was happy to answer.

"Yes! As soon as I've had my breakfast." I waved the green tea latte a little too enthusiastically and a couple of milky green drops sloshed out of the cup, spattering the werewolf's T-shirt. Again.

"I'm so sorry!" I gasped, deeply embarrassed. "Um. Is there anything I can do?"

But the werewolf shook his head. "Shop later," he said gruffly.

Did that mean he would go shopping later when he'd changed his clothes? Or that he'd come by the bookshop later? Surely he could use more than two words at a time. But before I could ask more, the person behind the counter asked pointedly "Next, please."

I was holding up the line. I hurried out, only too glad to make my escape from the werewolf I kept spilling things on.

Chapter Ten

It seemed I'd underestimated the demand for a magical bookshop. And it was a good thing I'd splurged on the sandwich earlier, because I was swamped as soon as I opened. Mundanes, wizards, trolls and more flooded in through the shop's door. The teen witches weren't part of the crowd, but then I'd judged them young enough to potentially still be at school. No doubt they'd appear later, or in the weekend.

My fears about a lack of sales were happily unfounded, and I silently blessed every minute I'd spent figuring out the vagaries of the cash register. Payments rolled in; mostly card transactions from the mundane humans, but I was also offered several jewels and some pieces of gold—not all in coins, either. One was a rough nugget that looked like it needed time in a smelter to render it into something valuable, but the cash register accepted it and gave rather a lot of change in exchange for the book on dwarven economics. I grimaced at the pile of obsidian discs it had disgorged into my hand, but the customer, who appeared to be some dwarf-human mixture, seemed happy enough. I decided I'd just have to trust the cash register on that one.

Around lunchtime I took cover *behind* the cash register, munching avocado and sourdough and feeling like a proper city dweller: I had a bought lunch and I was actually operating a shop! It took me a while to get through the sandwich, because every time I finished a bite, I looked up to find another customer was waiting. I was beginning to think I'd need to locate a stool to sit on in between customers; my feet were protesting the unaccustomed hours of standing around. At least I'd had plenty of things to keep my mind off my sore feet. I'd even had a roaming troll stop by and purchase all eight pink plastic flamingos. I gave him a bargain price: I was *very* happy to see evidence of my mistaken purchase being carried out the door.

The troll had supplied me with an uncut diamond in payment for the flamingoes (he also got a lot of change in smaller diamonds), and a brownie (the magical type, not the cake) had offered a gold coin for a book, giving me a sly look. I wasn't sure if brownie-gold was the same as faerie gold (which evaporated in the night), but I'd taken it in exchange for an (ironically) somewhat dusty book on housekeeping through the ages. I figured it wasn't a title that was likely to move fast based on both the existing dust, and the title. And with luck the cash register with its weird purple portals would deal with any monetary shenanigans in the night.

I'd just put the last bite of the sandwich in my mouth when a squeaking sound caught my ear. It was higher pitched than the hamster squeaks I'd been hearing for the last couple of days, and was worryingly near the corner where the grimoire lay. I took a card payment for a booklet about fossil-hunting in ghoul territory (a terrible idea, I couldn't help but think, but they say there's a sport for everyone), and then hurried back to the grimoire's section.

A bat was flittering around the grimoire, which had once again managed to launch itself onto the floor—unless of course, someone had taken it out. I looked suspiciously at the bat. It was daylight outside, even if the interior of the bookshop was on the dim side despite all the lights on. There *shouldn't* be a bat out and about. It was probably squeaking, though I couldn't hear it. The grimoire was *definitely* squeaking, via the music player, and on a frequency I could hear. *Did that mean the bat couldn't hear it*, I wondered wildly as I looked between bat and grimoire? *Actually...* I corrected myself. As I looked between *vampire* bat and grimoire.

"There aren't enough spiders left in here to warrant a bat coming in for them," I commented, deciding that it was probably best to be diplomatic on my first day as a bookseller. "So I'm assuming that's not what you're here for. Can you please stop bothering my... book?"

The vampire bat did a full circle around the grimoire, and I held up a hand and injected a bit more sternness into my tone. "No forming portals or scrying flights either, thank you."

There's a lot that can be done with triple circles widdershins by a knowledgeable practitioner, and

I wasn't keen for any of those things to happen in my bookshop, and especially not to the grimoire. I felt a certain responsibility towards it, even if it was grumpy and demanding.

The vampire/bat hovered, somehow conveying an air of sulkiness. Then it arrowed for the bookcase behind the grimoire and started tugging at another book. Another grimoire perhaps? Or was it one of the books I'd been reading to the grimoire? I wasn't sure, because the bat's small body and wings obscured the spine. In any case, I didn't want any of my books damaged by claws or teeth.

I cast about, wondering what I could do about a bat in a bookshop. In principle bats were fine, but not when they started biting books—and especially not when they were really disguised vampires. I didn't have any handy stakes (those on the flamingos had been taken out the door some time ago), and the vampire hadn't actually tried to drain anyone of blood. What else was a good weapon against vampires? I had garlic upstairs, but I didn't want to leave the bookshop unattended. That left me with holy water and sunlight. Sunlight was hard to come by in the shop, what with the lack of windows. And I didn't have holy water. Only a bit of leftover green tea.

I've got to try something...

I raced through the aisles to get the tea, and did a sort of flattened run back, holding the tea out in front of me to keep it from splashing about. Removing the lid from my new earthenware travel cup, I dipped my fingers into the foamy green stuff and, careful to avoid any droplets touching the grimoire, I let three drops of green tea latte drip onto the wildly flapping vampire bat.

It might just have been a reaction to the now-cold tea on its back, or perhaps vampires (or vampire bats) aren't keen on L-theanine (an active component in green tea, as I had learned from one of the books I'd reshelved). Whatever the reason, the green tea latte had an instant effect. The bat disappeared in a dark haze, and reformed into a tall, thin—no, *cadaverous*—man wrapped in a long black cloak with three drops of green foam on its collar. Actually, I only inferred that he was tall, as he was hunched over and holding onto the book that the bat had latched onto. He set the book down and stood up, confirming my suspicions about his height and vampirism. No-one but a vampire could look quite that close to dead without actually being so. I took an involuntary step back and he smiled in an unpleasantly predatory way.

"My apologies, dear lady," he said.

I wondered if he ever cut his tongue on those protruding fangs.

"I assume you want to purchase a book?" I asked, my tone as pointed as his fangs. The bat he'd been hadn't showed any signs of wanting to purchase. Steal, possibly. Though to be fair, it hadn't had a chance to take the book to the cash register in the middle of the shop.

"Perhaps I could browse a little first?" he suggested. "There is a great deal to choose from in this shop, after all."

I started to cross my arms and realised I'd spill the tea if I did so. Instead, I took the last sip and set the cup on the floor for now. *Then* I crossed my arms. "How about you tell me what you were looking for, and I can direct you to that section." I was quite proud of how many books I'd managed to reorganise in one short week. No doubt I'd missed some, but at least I now knew roughly where everything was, and I'd fixed some of the more egregious shelving issues.

"Ah... Well, if you must know, I would dearly love to purchase this lovely book here." He gestured at the grimoire, which flipped its pages. Was it being inviting? Sarcastic? Screaming no with all its might? I couldn't tell. But it had belonged to Kath, and had cooled my burnt hands after I'd helped banish the elemental in the forest. I wasn't parting with it to some random vampire.

"It's not for sale," I snapped.

"But it *is* in a bookshop."

It was hard to argue with that. I tried, anyway. "It needs company. So it's down here with the other books." There, that didn't sound mad at all, did it?

"In that case, perhaps I could keep it company from time to time. You must be busy with all the customers in here." Perhaps sensing my disbelief, the vampire held up a skeletal hand. "No, no, I am perfectly sincere. You must understand, living practically forever, as one does"—he gestured to himself"—one does not have the resources to purchase such fine books with impunity. One might think that compound interest on investments would mean all vampires are rich, but that does not take into account the mounting costs of undeath, you see."

I raised an enquiring eyebrow, not quite sure what to make of the unexpected flood of information.

"Daylight, my dear. One must have insurance. And undisturbed vaults are as much in demand in this city as," he shuddered, "trendy bars. Although those do make good hunting grounds." He paused to lick his lips, making *me* shudder. Apparently the city was more dangerous than I'd imagined. I privately vowed to stay out of any vault-like bars if and when I explored the city's nightlife.

"I've heard enough," I said before he could continue. "I don't need any hunters in my store."

I would have continued, but the grimoire riffled its pages loudly.

I peered down at the pages when they stilled. Sure enough, a poem had appeared.

> *Sanguine seeker though he be*
> *This one should not make you flee*
> *A companion I seek*
> *Not a vampiric freak*
> *Yet tales told by such as he*
> *Might yet manage to divert me*

I sighed. Trumped by a book.

"Apparently the grimoire doesn't mind if you stay." I grimaced. "But no stealing books, and you can only stay here during opening hours. If you get in the way of other customers, you're going out. Got it?" I tried not to wonder what I would do if he *did* overstay his welcome. Maybe I could find a good book of warding recipes to amp up what I already had.

"You're too kind."

I backed away from the vamp's wide, toothy smile. "Oh, and no hunting my customers."

The vamp hesitated, then bowed. "Very well. At least not on the premises."

I supposed that was as much as I could hope for.

'Bake with a pinch of regret.' I wrinkled my nose at the instruction. Regret was easy to feel—I was regretting choosing this recipe already—but getting a pinch of it into a spell? I was beginning to think I should just leave my wards as they were and accept the odd vamp visitor in the shop.

Then I imagined waking up to a vamp in my bedroom, and shuddered. I might accept a vamp as a customer, but there were limits. The chances seemed high that the missive I'd found slipped under the floor a few days ago was from the same vamp who had made an ally of my grimoire in the shop today.

I'd closed the shop at the end of the day footsore, but determined to take some precautions, and the book I'd found on wards had marked the one I was trying to construct as the best available. It called for granite pebbles, a smear of marmite, quite a lot of thyme, and the aforementioned pinch of regret, as well as a large quantity of vinegar and baking soda. It was considerably more esoteric than my usual wards. I rubbed my forehead with the hand that wasn't holding the mixing spoon. If I kept peering into obscure books with faded printing in poor light, I'd get a massive wrinkle there, glasses or no.

So... back to the recipe for stronger wards. I'd have to be practical. Regret could be expressed as tears, right? I concentrated on everything I'd been missing from home. No matter how deeply I'd felt the difference between me and my Seer family, they'd been everything I'd known for so long. Dad's cooking, Mum's hugs, even my sister's endless demands—it was so odd to be without them. I regretted leaving even while enjoying my newfound freedom. And the one person I'd met in this town—not counting the vamp, of course—hadn't showed up on my opening day. I'd rather hoped the werewolf would come, but he hadn't. A tear trickled down my cheek. I leaned forward and let it drop into my bowl. I gave the mix a final stir and carefully pressed the result into the moulds I'd made out of empty pudding bowls, purchased at the second-hand shop, ten for a dollar. It had been worth closing two minutes early to pick up the ward receptacles:

these wards were much messier than my simple herb-and-crystal ones.

Take that, vamp, I thought as I slid the glass bowls into the oven. *I can bake with regret any day.* If only I wasn't feeling so miserable about it. It was a good thing I had saved some of my brownies from earlier in the week. I served myself a piece of chocolatey goodness and sat down on the couch for a good wallow.

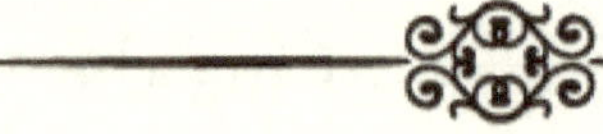

Chapter Eleven

The Customers

The first day I was open, I was too busy to pay much attention to the customers' conversations among themselves, but the next day, although foot traffic was still abundant, I was a trifle more relaxed. I walked through the aisles in between serving customers, tidying shelves and eavesdropping shamelessly.

"You call that a dog? Looks more like a mop with trust issues." The vamp was present again despite my beefed-up wards—but then, I'd placed those around my apartment. He was hanging around while I checked that yesterday's customers hadn't made a mess of my shelving system.

"Umm, I think it might actually be a werewolf," I said, looking down at the dog in question. It had long, rather bedraggled fur, and it was looking at the vamp warily. *Should I have a policy against pets in the bookshop?* But then people would have to leave them outside, and if it had been *my* dog, I wouldn't have wanted to do that. Plus, if it really was a werewolf, it was its choice what form it used. And without Rex here with me, I was happy to let other dogs in. No, better to leave things as they were. Besides, I could hardly blame it for the way it looked at the vamp. I probably looked at the vamp with distrust too. "I mean, I would have noticed if a dog walked in the door by itself." Especially one that looked like that, I thought but didn't say aloud. After all, I was supposed to be customer focused, and dissing a potential customer due to their appearance was surely not that.

I eyed the critical vamp, who was dressed in the classical vampire style of tuxedo, cape and broad-brimmed hat. Exactly why vamps had got stuck in the style of a couple of centuries back, I didn't know. But it wasn't a surprise that it was the aristocrat-meets-highwayman style that had caught their fancy. After all, vamps specialised in 'your money or your life'.

This particular vamp didn't seem to be in any hurry to part me from either, which was an unexpected blessing. He'd entered the shop first thing when I came downstairs this morning after my grand opening day yesterday. Presumably my new wards ensured that he could only come in with good intentions.

The shaggy dog pricked its ears at me, then sauntered back out the door, wariness apparently forgotten. Perhaps it really had been a werewolf.

Just not Dirk. Dirk was a better customer. I sighed, and chose another shelf to tidy, further away from the vamp, closer to the door. The sound of raised voices led me to the next aisle, where I encountered another couple of problematic customers. These ones were arguing with each other. *Should I swoop in and offer help with book selection to break it up?* I decided to wait until I knew what they were quarrelling about.

"I'm not saying you stole my cactus, but that's a suspicious number of needles on your jumper." The speaker was clearly a witch of the classical persuasion, based on her black clothing and silver jewellery.

The customer she was speaking to—probably the descendant of some sort of desert dweller, based on the suggestion of scales behind his ears, which weren't covered by his cap—straightened up to his full height, towering above me and the impudent (or did I mean imprudent?) young witch who'd accused him. Despite the late summer heat and humidity, he wore a knitted jumper with a roll neck and long, floppy sleeves. There were quite a number of needles which could conceivably belong to a cactus adorning the jumper.

"I would never steal." He stated it as a fact. Then he licked his lips, inadvertently displaying the masticated remains of a cactus. Not as bad as the vamp's fangs, but still not a sight I wanted to see while I sipped on my morning drink. There hadn't been any cactuses in the bookshop, so one of the customers must have brought one in.

"Eating someone else's cactus is as good as stealing!" The witch put her hands on her hips.

There was my cactus-bearer. I wondered why she'd bothered to bring one. It seemed an odd book-shopping accessory.

The tall, cactus-eating customer lowered his eyebrows and glared menacingly at her, then began to puff out neck pouches I hadn't spotted under the roll-neck jumper.

Oh, great. Looks like he's one of those Chaldean scorpion men from the desert. Gaia only knows what he's doing here, you'd think it's far too humid, and not nearly hot enough. Still, time to intervene, before someone gets a poison spine in the arm.

"Excuse me," I asked the witch. "Can I interest you in a... a... a book on mythological desert creatures?" I was grasping at straws, but I didn't need a murder on my hands, and either the witch or the lanky scorpion-man might commit one at this rate.

"No, thank you." The witch didn't take her eyes off the scorpion-man.

"You could browse the latest catalogue of crystal balls?" I tried to think what else might appeal to a witch who carried cacti into a bookshop. "Er, or perhaps plants are your interest?" I had *shelves* of books on plants, both magical and otherwise.

Finally I'd caught her attention. "Yes. I need something on brewing from succulents. You know, agave, saguaro, Barbary fig, that sort of thing." She shot a glare at the cactus-eater. "I *did* bring in a sample of the one I need recipes for, but one of your customers *nibbled* it."

I bit my lip, trying not to laugh. It was wrong to laugh at customers, wasn't it? It might only be my second day on the job, but I was pretty sure about that rule.

"That's... terrible. I know we have a lot of recipe books. They're all over this way, let me show you." I ushered the witch over to the bulging recipe-book shelves, safely away from the cactus-eater. I might have to consider a sale on the recipe section before long, just to clear things out a bit. "If you can't find what you're looking for, let me know. I might be able to order something in." I made the offer without thinking, then realised I'd have to do some research on book ordering. That was probably overdue anyway: I'd need to be able to replace books as I sold them.

The witch was silent for a few minutes, scanning the shelves. Then she seemed to register my words.

"That's fine, I think I've found what I needed." She held up a book I didn't even remember shelving: 'Brewing with Spite & Spine'. There *was* a picture of some sort of cactus on the cover.

"I'm so glad," I said with feeling. I tried to remember that as she haggled with me on the price, trying for a fifty percent discount. "This is only my second day open," I explained, again. "And that's a valuable book." I pointed to the hand-written price on the inside cover. "I could sell it to another witch at twice that price online. And it's out of print, so I can't replace it." I'd found that out when I tried a quick internet search to see if she was correct in her evaluation of its worth.

"Oh, very well then," she agreed at last. As she counted out notes from what looked like a solid silver case, I caught a glimpse of larger denominations inside. The slight feeling that I was being unreasonable dissipated. Whatever this witch did with cacti, she wasn't hurting for cash.

I didn't find out what the scorpion-man wanted, because he left the shop without purchasing anything shortly after the witch had bought her book. I just hoped they didn't encounter each other anywhere else. Still, at least it wouldn't be my problem if they did.

The customer who *did* surprise me was the werewolf I'd encountered on the bus and in the bakery. He showed up just before closing time, hauling a couple of heavy-looking grocery bags with him.

"Recipes?" he asked.

I grinned, partly because I *didn't* have any green tea to spill on him this time, partly because I was happy to sell more recipe books. It was kind of nice to see a familiar face, too. It had only been a few days since I'd left home, but it was very… different, not being surrounded by people I knew. Both good and bad. I could do whatever I wanted, and no-one would know if it was in character or not. On the other hand, I had no-one to talk to who wasn't a customer.

"Absolutely. I have a lot for you to choose from." Once again I led the way to the relevant section, glancing towards the back corner where the vamp had been hanging out. He hadn't buy a book today, but he'd bought enough yesterday for me to consider my decision to allow him in as a good one. He was still there now, but he'd shelved his latest tome and looked to be on his way out. Good. I couldn't feel completely relaxed with a vamp in the shop, no matter how many wards I had. The werewolf looked too. I thought he growled a little, but the grimoire flipped the music just then to 'The Blue Danube'. Somehow it had figured out the volume controls too, because the saccharine tones echoed through the shop.

"Sorry about the music," I yelled to the werewolf.

He gave me a wry, amused look, as though he knew it wasn't to my taste, then turned his attention to the books.

"Sugar-free?" he asked, raising his voice to be heard.

Shaking my head at the thought of a life without sugar, I thumbed through the books until I found a couple that might fit the request: 'Artificial Sweeteners for the Modern Werewolf', and 'No Sugar, No Spice, Nothing Tastes Nice'. I wasn't sure about the second book; it was hardly selling itself with its title. It could have been about just about anything, and I'd run out of time to flip through it before opening the shop. Feeling that I needed to prove myself, I searched on through the recipe books. Surely there was something relevant I'd seen? Yes, there it was: a book entitled simply 'Carnivorous', with a bloody-looking piece of meat on the marbled red and white cover. That should suit a werewolf, surely? And it seemed unlikely that there were sugary recipes in it. But I glanced between the book and the werewolf's grocery bags, and hesitated. There looked to be a lot of vegetables in those bags. Maybe I was on the wrong track.

"Did you have any other requirements?" I asked doubtfully.

The werewolf returned my earlier grin, displaying teeth that rivaled those of the vamp.

Yes, that's why I thought carnivorous. My eyes got rather stuck on those teeth.

There was a movement behind me, and I whipped around to see the vamp in question showing his teeth right back at the werewolf.

I was dimly aware that the background music had changed from classical to a thumping rendition of 'Wild Thing'. I was going to have to have a word with that grimoire.

But first, I needed to prevent inter-species warfare inside my bookshop.

"It's about time for you to head out, isn't it?" I said to the vampire with a glance outside. It wasn't yet dark, but he had left the shop at a similar time yesterday, well wrapped up in his cloak and hood.

"I trust you will be careful with the lycanthrope," the vamp said with a sneer and a look at the werewolf.

"I'm just showing him books," I said firmly.

The vamp gave me a sardonic nod and edged around us. He didn't seem keen to get too close to the werewolf.

I wasn't sure what that meant for my own safety but at least neither of them lunged at the other before the vamp made his way out of the shop.

Slightly relieved, I turned my attention back to the werewolf, whose teeth were no longer showing.

"Eggplant."

"Sorry?" I thought I must have misheard him.

"Many eggplants." He lifted one of the grocery bags and opened it to show me that it was indeed full of purple-black, glossy eggplants. Perhaps he'd got a good deal at the fruit shop.

"Oh. Right. Well, I can't imagine those taste good when candied. Um... here you are." I skipped over the meat-based books in favour of one with an eggplant and a bunch of chilli peppers on its cover, entitled simply 'Aubergine.' I hadn't had a chance to glance through that one either, but it looked like a good bet.

The werewolf—Dirk, I remembered his name was—took the book and flipped through it. To my surprise he reddened and shut it hastily.

"Wrong section," he growled, handing it back to me.

I opened the book on a page at random and also closed it quickly. "Oh. Ah. Yes, I see. Sorry." It had definitely been mis-shelved. In the wrong bookshop. Suffice to say that the illustrations hadn't been of vegetables.

I put the offending book on a high shelf, as high as I could reach, and grabbed another book—one I had actually read, because it reminded me of home.

"How about something Greek? Lots of eggplant recipes in there." I tried to ignore my own blushing face.

"Yes," Dirk said. He was clearly a wolf of few words. Back in the pine forest I'd thought the smoke might have been affecting his throat, but that clearly wasn't the case.

"You must be feeding a lot of people." There were surely more eggplants in that one grocery bag than one person could eat.

"Yes. Pack Chef." This time his smile didn't show any teeth. My heart beat faster anyway. Or possibly that was just the latest tune the grimoire had switched to: a flamenco guitar version of '*Flight of the Bumblebee*'. It seemed we were back to classical.

"That must keep you busy," I said inanely. "Will the Greek cookbook work out?"

"Will try."

Wonderful. At least it looked like I had a sale, despite my embarrassing blunder with the wrong book.

The teenage witches who'd been waiting for me to open didn't come in until late on Saturday, but when they did appear, they were enthusiastic.

"OMG, I can't believe you have the OG *Silencio Tarot* guide," one gushed. "My mum used to talk about that one." She let go of the other teen's hand long enough to flick through the pages, pausing frequently to admire the illustrations in the guide.

"Didn't you say you had to do a reading?" I asked, remembering our conversation outside the shop before I'd opened.

"Yeah, but I took your tip about the pendulum and used that instead. Good thing, because it was a total hands off situation."

I nodded as though I had a clue what she meant.

"So that means I'm left with a bike I need to sell, like yesterday," she said, as though in explanation.

"You need just to list it for sale. It's not like the curse is transferable," her companion said glibly.

"Only if you believe my brother," the witch muttered. "Would you?"

I moved the conversation along, not wanting to get bogged down in discussions of curses *or* bicycles. Definitely not cursed bicycles.

"Did you want to see the rest of the tarot decks? I found several while I was organising," I suggested.

"Yes please." The one swathed in black had forgone the eyelashes today, but laid on a heavy coating of eyeliner to make up for that lack, covering even the waterline in black gunk. My eyes watered in sympathy, but they didn't seem bothered. Perhaps that was just a me thing. I'd never been much into makeup. I told myself I had to stop judging people on their appearance. After all, I was in a customer-facing role now, unlike my past life in researching for Seers.

Then again, it was hard *not* to make assumptions about people. Based on appearance alone, I was guessing that this customer would fall in love with the tarot selection I'd found, which leaned heavily to moons, bones, and hand-drawn crystal shards.

It was the jeans-clad witch who oohed and aahed, however. The one in black asked if I had a catalogue of runestones, so I promised to get one in. I hadn't found any of those in my days of stocktaking.

Still, both witches left with a small stack of guidebooks, including one as a gift, and I felt like I'd pleased the pair. They promised to come back next week to see if the runestone book had arrived, and asked if I'd order in the runestones themselves if they found one they liked.

"Yes, I can do that," I assured them. That was something I'd done myself, more than once, in my quest to be able to See anything at all. My failure didn't mean they wouldn't have more success.

"I'll tell Mum's coven that you've opened the bookshop again. They've been complaining about the lack of decent shops to buy spell books," the black-clad teen assured me. "And maybe you could get some games in, too? My brother's into board games, he would totes come in if you had games."

"That's a great suggestion, thank you," I agreed.

"And if you're new in town, you should know that the traffic is the absolute worst. You should get a bike to get around," they assured me.

Tucking their cash into the cash register's purple glow, I gave the pair a genuine smile before turning to help the next customer. Perhaps I *should* consider getting a bike. But not from either of the teens. Just in case.

Chapter Twelve

A DAY OFF

The next day was a Sunday. I'd made the decision to close on Sundays so that I had at least one day to explore my new home, not to mention a day to recover from the constant onslaught of people. Back in my tiny hometown, of *course* we still had contact with others—but mostly, that was with people we knew. I'd looked forward to meeting new people wherever I ended up, but the change was like going from drinking from a dripping tap to trying to sip from a fire hydrant. Plus, my feet had started sending me signals of protest half-way through Saturday. They'd still been sore this morning, making me think I might need to invest in better shoes, too. A break was non-negotiable.

In my exploration of the shop's contents I'd found a somewhat torn map, unsuitable for sale. The old map had ragged edges and a tear through the middle of it, obscuring the only place name on it. After a bit of investigation, the bookshop yielded a series of maps, and I eventually matched up the coastline on the old map and one of the newer ones. It looked like it was a nearby beach, one I could reach by bus. A beach seemed like a good escape from the confines of the windowless bookshop.

Equipped with the map, a swimsuit from the secondhand shop, and an all-day bus ticket, I set out to explore. The first hitch in my plan became obvious when I had to wait an hour for a bus that would take me in the right direction. Apparently city people didn't take buses on a Sunday—at least not in this city. Still, I had time and patience (and a book to read), so I sat on a bench and waited for the bus. Unlike waiting for the bus in my hometown, there were no water sprites to amuse me when my attention strayed from the book.

Probably, I should have selected something more exciting than a treatise on the interaction of earth spirits and volcanic eruptions, but it had seemed like something I should know about, given the city was built on a volcanic field. But I did spot a wind elemental twirling around the fronds of a palm tree further along the street. I made a mental note to check that I'd included the right crystals in my wards to prevent entry by elementals when I returned to the bookshop. A wind elemental would play havoc with the books. This one became bored and disappeared into the clouds before long, so I was able to relax (and wish the breeze it had brought would return; it was another hot and muggy day) until the bus finally pulled up at the stop.

The map had prompted me to visit the beach, but once I arrived, I wished I had company. Tāmaki Makaurau, Auckland, might be a huge city compared to the rural hamlet I'd come from, but when you didn't know any one of the one and a half million or so inhabitants, it might as well be empty.

Leaving my towel draped over my bag on the sandy shore, I tiptoed through the gauntlet of mud and oyster shells that separated the sand from the water (next time I'd check when high tide was, so I could swim straight from the sandy beach), and submerged myself.

The relief from the city's humid warmth made the expedition immediately worthwhile, though I kept imagining sharks and jellyfish, and my feet were muddied and a little cut from the shells by the time I reached the sand again. I rubbed the mud off with sand, and sat reading for a while on the beach while I dried off. However, although the day wasn't bright, there was enough sun to glare off the pages of my book and give me a headache. I was also getting peckish, but I could put off food for a while. Especially since I'd discovered that the bakery on the corner was also closed on a Sunday, so I had no thrilling treats to tempt me to eat early.

Not sure what to do next, I made my way back to the bus stop and took the next bus that came along. Once again, I had to wait a long time. Maybe I really should invest in a bicycle. The bus took me towards the central city, but I decided to get off before it crossed the harbour bridge. I had the feeling I'd need more cash and less sand scratching my sandaled feet for a city visit. I spotted a park and pushed the bus's stop button.

It looked like as good a place as any to explore, and no-one could mind sandy feet in a park.

The park's welcome sign had been painted over to say 'Run while you can.' The paint dripped off the sign, still wet. Puddles of white paint formed underneath it, mixed with green from the freshly mown grass. The reek of fresh paint filled the air. Whoever had done it had been in a hurry, and very liberal with their paint. But why? And possibly more importantly, what should I (or whoever the sign was aimed at) be running from? I glanced around, suddenly uneasy. The park was in a sort of bowl surrounded by a low hill. Houses topped the hill, but there was native bush below them. Beyond the sign, a wrought iron gate swooped in fanciful patterns, and ducks swam on a pond beyond that. Grass carpeted the ground, the suggestion of a wetland beyond the pond. It was a nice reminder of home that I hadn't expected, given how developed the city was, and certainly didn't suggest anything to run from. Perhaps the graffiti was just the work of bored teens.

Shouts and yells in the distance suggested either the presence of children or an ongoing supernatural battle. I hoped it was the former; with no ability to See, hoping was the best I could do. Besides, this was a park; surely a playground was more likely than a battle. I looked around. Sure enough, in the distance small people in colourful clothing shouted and screamed at each other. Typical playground warfare. Satisfied that there was no reason for me to get involved, I returned my attention to the painted-over sign.

Afternoon sun glistened on the paint, so I should be safe from vamps, who never went out in broad daylight. That left... just about everything else. A flurry of movement made me cast a suspicious look towards a shrub near the sign, but it was just a troupe of silvereyes, the small birds passing through in search of insects, their tiny green wings flicking open and closed as they used the least possible energy to stay in constant motion. A couple of pixies followed them, bounding through the thin branches. I wasn't sure if the pixies were chasing the birds or just following them in the hope that they stirred up something tasty. Either way, they all ignored me.

The presence of the birds and pixies meant there probably wasn't a serious predator nearby, and I relaxed a little. Still, I didn't feel like lingering any longer. It looked like there were wetlands in the distance: just the sort of place swamp dragons might nest. I had no desire to repeat my previous near-death experience with a swamp dragon. Instead, I crossed the road in order to catch a bus in a new direction. I wasn't done exploring, but it was time to go and find some food.

The next bus to come along took me through more suburbs to another suburban centre, this one with a long line of shops backing on to the reserve behind the beach, many of them restaurants with beach bars. The moment I saw an entire shop devoted to ice cream, I decided that ice cream was a perfectly reasonable lunch. Especially since it also sold ice cream sundaes, with layers of fruit sandwiched between the ice-cream. That made it practically healthy, right? I took my chocolate-sauce-drenched green-tea-and-pomegranate ice cream lunch onto the grassy slope that led to the beach, and found a shady tree with wide boughs to sit under while I ate. The ground was carpeted with dull red stamens from what must have been a spectacular flowering season. It was odd to think that if things worked out with the bookshop, I could be seeing the next round of flowers here in a year's time.

Gentle waves made a shushing sound as they rippled up the beach, and I finally had a good view of Rangitoto, the massive volcano that dominated the harbour. I wondered what my book would have to say about such a bold volcano, but couldn't quite muster the enthusiasm to dig it out to find out. Besides, the local seagulls had realised I was eating and gathered around me, cawing at each other in strident tones. Someone paddled past on a board, standing high over the water. I stared, fascinated, until a sudden wave sloshed over their paddleboard. I blinked a couple of times. I was almost sure I'd seen an iridescent tail swooshing that wave into being. Perhaps I needed to look up water deities and associated fauna as well as volcanoes. All in all, it was a good thing the bookshop was so well-stocked. Just in case the unseen denizens of this beach were dangerous, I decided I'd leave any further swimming for another occasion. I finished my sundae and placed the evidence in a bin before the gulls could get too enthusiastic. Without a Seer on hand to tell me how risky an activity was, I was going to have to reassess my approach to risk analysis.

While this beach was further from the bookshop, it might be nice to return to it from time to time, even if I didn't enter the water. On the way to finding my ice cream, I'd spotted a Thai restaurant I wouldn't mind getting dinner from at some point, and there was no mud between the sand and the sea here. I decided I had better walk off my meal before I left the seaside, and set off along the curving beach towards the cliff at the far end, leaving the disappointed gulls behind.

I walked along the beach and back, shells crunching under my sandals with every step. But these weren't oyster shells; my feet were relatively safe. The clouds had parted since I'd left the first beach, and the sun sparkled on the edge of every gently breaking wave. It was a glorious day.

All the same, I wasn't entirely happy. I kept wishing I had Rex by my side. Lots of other people had their dogs with them. I was fairly sure some of the dogs were actually werewolves, based on size alone. Although, perhaps werewolves wouldn't allow themselves to be leashed. Still, none came near me. Thoughts of my lost dog spoiled my enjoyment of the day, no matter that my Seer family had assured me that he was safe, somewhere. I wondered if they'd let me know when he turned up, or if my abrupt departure meant I was on my own as far as they were concerned? With my lack of skill in the Seeing department, only time would tell. Given my younger sister had already sent one letter, timed to arrive before me at the bookshop, I'd be amazed if she could keep herself from meddling.

As I returned along the beach, the shadows from trees and fancy houses lengthened and a cool evening breeze blew in off the sea. It was time to head back to the bookshop.

Chapter Thirteen

The bus home had been uneventful—until now.

"I told you not to press that red button, and what did you do?" The bus driver was engaged in a heated argument with the button-presser, who appeared to be of dwarven persuasion—iron helmet, beard-plaits, and kilt all present and correct. Also, a very nasty temper. I gazed at the emergency exit and wondered if now was the moment to use the small hammer housed over the window, and smash the glass. Perhaps not.

After all, the dwarf's chief concern seemed to be whether or not the driver would make an extra stop at the pub.

"The button is what you press when you want to get off, innit?" he demanded

"And I'll stop when we get to a bus stop," the driver insisted.

The dwarf reached over his shoulder, and I realised he probably had an axe slung over his back, given his traditional attire.

"Oh no, matey, don't do that." The bus driver—still driving rather faster than I thought was wise on the traffic-filled road, especially since his eyes were focused on the rear-view mirror—raised his voice in warning. "All you need to do is wait, and then walk. The pub is a hundred metres past the stop after next. You could crawl it if you had to."

"I don't wanna walk," the dwarf grumped. "That's why I'm on a bus, right?" He hadn't stopped fiddling with the straps on his shoulder, and I feared that violence was imminent. Someone had to do something.

I reached deep inside, and found… the customer service voice I'd been developing with every day that I worked in the bookshop.

"What is it you're going to drink when you get to the pub?" I asked the irate dwarf, polite interest dripping from my words. Not an original topic, but I was grasping at straws for what to say.

He turned in his seat to look at me, eyes blinking in the harsh lights of the bus. "What's it to you?"

I recoiled inwardly, but I'd started this conversation so I could get to my own bus stop in safety, so I'd have to continue it.

"Just curious what the locals drink," I said lamely. "I'm new in town." Back home, people drank beer, or if they were my parents, retsina (when they could get hold of it) or ouzo. The fancier folks opted for chardonnay from the vineyards down the valley, claiming (perhaps correctly) that they were supporting the local economy. I was betting the dwarf would be a beer drinker. Probably stout. But he surprised me.

"The pub I'm going to does the best espresso martinis on this side of the bridge. Their Cosmopolitan isn't bad either, for an old fashioned drink." His grumpy face eased into a dreamy smile. "Just the thing after a good axe-throwing session."

I couldn't let that go without comment.

"There's axe-throwing in the city?"

"Oh, aye, just on from th'pub. A nice wee underground club. But there's a no drinking before throwing policy. So maybe I'll go for a quick throw first."

It seemed like a sound policy to have, but I didn't want to rile the dwarf. I segued. "I've never tried a martini. Doesn't the coffee keep you awake?"

"Aye, it does, but that means there's more time to party." The dwarf gave me a knowing wink.

I tried to avoid imagining what a post-axe-throwing-and-espresso-martini party might entail, but failed. Was it something like the parties my parents held when they managed to round up a few friends who shared their Greek heritage, with endless meze and apparently limitless ouzo? Not to mention dancing. They never held one of those parties before an important forecasting day. My curiosity went into overdrive.

"Do you take your axe partying, too?" I couldn't help but ask. The dwarf looked affronted.

"Naturally I do." Then he deflated. "Though the bouncers make me check it in with the coats if I hit the nightclubs."

Wise bouncers.

At that moment the bus lurched to a halt. I peered out into the street and realised that we'd reached my stop. Someone else must be getting off here too, as I hadn't thought to press the button, preoccupied as I'd been by the dwarf.

"Enjoy your axe-throwing," I said politely to the dwarf as I hurried down the aisle to exit the bus. An middle-aged woman got off in front of me and walked off towards the cluster of restaurants. No doubt heading out to dinner.

"That I will," the dwarf agreed with a chuckle. Apparently my brief conversation with him had settled his ire, because as I stepped off the bus, he called in an almost civil tone to the driver.

"Full speed ahead to the next stop, my man. My axe needs a workout."

Shaking my head at such capricious behavior, I made my way back to the bookshop. Perhaps I could locate a book of cocktails and try making my own martini. Or even a Cosmopolitan, that sounded like something a city girl should try.

Chapter Fourteen

THE GRIMOIRE

I was met with the sound of silence. Literally, that is; the song echoed around the bookshop as I opened the door and slipped inside. Locking the door behind me, I briefly rested my head against it. This thing with the grimoire was getting old. Although I did sympathise—I was feeling lonely myself—I still wasn't a fan of the wildly varying music selections the spell book came up with.

"All right, I'm back. Can you turn the music down a little?" I shouted.

The music whispered into nothingness and I made my way towards the staircase at the back of the shop that led to my apartment. There was a scuttling noise on top of one of the bookshelves and I swung around hastily, but failed to see the source of the noise. Perhaps the hamsters were out and about. I made a mental note to add hamster food to my shopping list. If I fed them appropriately, in a place of my choosing, maybe they would leave my books and pastries alone.

Fortunately, the grimoire wasn't generating smoke this time, so at least I could see and breathe as I approached it.

"I guess you need more than just a vampire reading to you during the day," I said.

It flipped its pages discontentedly. That seemed to mean yes.

"I know today was probably slow for you, but I need to get away from the bookshop from time to time," I explained. Predictably enough, the music player started up again, this time playing that Beatles classic, 'Eleanor Rigby'. Dad was a big Beatles fan, so I knew most of the music by heart—enough so that I didn't need to listen to the whole song to get the point. "Yes, I know you're lonely. I'm working on it." I softened my tone. "I'm lonely too, you know. I don't know anyone in this town. And yes, I chose to come here, but it's still hard work when everything you know changes." I sat down beside the grimoire. "How about we go easy on each other while we find our feet?" I suggested.

'Eleanor Rigby' faded smoothly into 'I don't want a lover'. I wasn't sure who the singer was, but the meaning was clear. I snorted with laughter. "Yeah, good call," I told the book. "Let's be friends."

The grimoire flipped its pages over again, and this time it lay open on another poem and the music faded away. I tapped on my phone's flashlight so as to read it more easily. It was too much like work to find my glasses in my beach bag.

> *Some like it hot,*
> *Some like it cold,*
> *The leprechaun visitor*
> *Is after your gold.*

"What?" I'd been expecting something lyrical about loneliness, friendship, or something else along those lines. Not a poetic warning about a customer. I thought quickly. "Is he in the building now?" I asked. Somehow talking to a book (rhymes and sound track optional) had become a perfectly normal part of my daily life. Once again, pages turned of their own accord.

> *Deep underneath*
> *He searches*
> *Always hunting*

Never finding
Rainbow gold
At days' ending.

That tracked, I guess. Leprechauns did like gold, and if the gold they sought was at the end of the rainbow... But my gold? I didn't think I had any. Well, other than the gold I'd taken from the brownie the other day. Perhaps that was it. I bit my lip, pondering the problem.

"The gold from the till?" I asked.

The pages flipped again. *Yes.*

I thought some more.

"Is it a problem right now? Do I need to move it? Or can I wait until the morning for a bank to open?"

The pages of the grimoire lay open for a few moments. I decided it was pondering the problem, or perhaps conducting some magical test that didn't show. Just when I'd decided I'd have to try and move the cash register to my room to keep it safe for the night, the music player sprang into life again. This time, it was playing a show tune: '*Tomorrow*', from the musical Annie.

"Thank goodness for that. I'll open late tomorrow, so I can find a bank for the gold first."

The grimoire closed with a snap, and I imagined it exuded a satisfied air.

"Thanks for the warning," I told it. "I'll have another go at finding you a companion tomorrow too."

Music started playing again, and it took me a few minutes to recognise Carole King singing 'You've got a friend'. I smiled, and stood up.

"Thanks. You too, I guess."

Despite the threat of thievery and the occasional scuttling sound from the hamsters, I slept well.

Chapter Fifteen

BANKING AND WIZARDRY

The elevator refused to stop on the thirteenth floor. I stabbed at the 'door open' button as the floor indicator light switched directly from 12 to 14. Nothing in my small-town experience had prepared me for unruly elevators, yet here I was stuck in one. I'd travelled back across the harbour bridge into the skyscraper-filled city, in order to add my name to the bookshop bank account. At this rate I'd be stuck hiding money, gold coins, and assorted supernatural currencies under my mattress for the foreseeable future.

I'd found the the cash register regurgitated its assorted currencies when I powered everything down for the night.

My finger hesitated over the elevator's alarm button. I didn't want to cause a fuss unless I really had to. But it wasn't looking good. Unless... surely there would be a staircase? I accepted level 14, and emerged into a bland carpeted hallway that felt utterly foreign to my existence thus far. I looked up and down the hall, and spotted a heavy door towards one end, with a green emergency exit sign above it. That must be the stairs. My feet made no sound on the thick carpet, and no-one appeared as I pushed the heavy glass door open. It was easy to imagine that the whole building was deserted. I reached the thirteenth floor through another heavy door, and was met with a reception desk. A dark-haired, dark-skinned man looked up with a smile as I entered.

"Can I help you?"

"I'm looking for…" I pulled the bank's business card (something that I'd found tucked into the grimoire this morning) out of my pocket. "Shadowfell Secure Bank."

"You've found it." The man smiled again. "Do you have an account?"

"Er, no. But I'd like to open one. I'm working for a bookshop that has dealt with your bank before." I had a perfectly good bank account from working in my family's financial futures business, but it seemed like a good idea to keep that separate from the bookshop finances. Who knew if Kath and Ron, the witch and wizard who'd gifted me the shop, would one day change their mind about retiring to cruise the islands in search of new adventures? If that happened, it would be easier to show them what I'd been doing with the place if I had a separate bank account. I just had to overcome the immediate challenge of opening one.

"No problem, I'll just need your government-issued ID, your business and personal address, a tax number, any income and expense evidence you may have, any debts invoked by moonlight, starlight or the in between, declaration of non-portal trading status, blood type and donation status..."

As his voice droned on, I wondered with rising panic how anyone ever managed to open a bank account in this town.

Three hours later, I walked out the door of the building with my bank account secured. Now all I had to do was transfer the gold, jewels, and whatever else was offered as currency on a weekly basis. I smiled with relief. Compared with sorting out the banking system, running a magical bookshop was going to feel easy.

Two hours after that, I wondered if I'd been correct about the ease of running a bookshop of any type.

"If you're going to lie about being a wizard, maybe don't use a wand with the price tag still on it," I said firmly as I backed away slowly from the pair of customers. I stopped when I bumped into a bookcase. I hadn't realised life in a bookshop would be quite so exciting. Or so dangerous. Although in this case, the danger was hopefully more to the wannabe wizard, rather than to me. Wands can backfire easily, when wielded by someone who doesn't know what they are doing. At least, so the witches who'd been chatting in the store earlier had told me. While Seers are sometimes regarded as a sub-branch of witches,

Seers don't use wands, and I wasn't familiar with their intricacies.

But no matter how little I knew about them, there was no way I wanted to be caught between an unregistered wizard wielding a wand, and a real wizard. There might even be newts, if the guy with the price-tagged wand didn't watch the way he was waving it. Imported wands are notorious for producing newts. I'd heard that the biosecurity folks were trying to ban such imports for the good of local biodiversity. In fact, that gave me an idea. Reaching behind me, I grabbed a large book which jutted out further than the others, ruining my display but making it easy to grab.

"Stop right there," I said, brandishing 'Air and Water: A guide to native frogs' like a shield between the two wizards, who were facing off over a book of elementary spells. It was a good thing neither of them had found the grimoire, which was uncharacteristically silent and still. "You need to make sure you're conjuring appropriate species."

Both the registered wizard and the wannabe-wizard turned to me with matching confused expressions.

"For what reason?" the registered wizard asked haughtily, dusting an imaginary speck of dust off his cloak, then adjusting the pin which identified him as a wizard in good standing with the guild.

"Yeah, what he said," the unregistered wizard echoed.

"Because there are hefty penalties, up to and including a jail sentence, for releasing unauthorised species in this country. Don't you cover biosecurity in wizard school? And you really don't want to get on the wrong side of Biosecurity, do you?"

"Those bumbling red-tape wielders? How would they even find out?" The registered wizard narrowed his eyes at me.

"Well, the book you're arguing over only contains a spell for 'a plague of frogs,'" I pointed out helpfully. It was a good thing I'd been interested in the contents of that book and read through it in my apartment last night. "If you use that spell, there's going to be a *lot* of evidence."

The haughty registered wizard looked suddenly thoughtful. The wannabe wizard shuffled quietly away behind another bookshelf, pocketing his wand as he did so.

"I'll take this book," the remaining wizard announced. "To keep it out of uneducated hands." He hesitated. "And perhaps that book about frogs, too." I was happy to help relieve him of his excess of cash in exchange for the two books. Perhaps he'd shut the spell book away in some sort of wizard's tower, but that was just typical wizardly behaviour, according to the tales my parents used to tell.

Later, the wannabe wizard ambled up to the cash register. "D'you have any more basic books on wizardry?" he asked.

I bit my lip. I had actually located several such books in my general stocktake, but there was a reason most wizards went through university. Learning spells without understanding the theory behind them often led to unexpected, if not fatal, results. "I'll keep an eye out for one," I temporised. I didn't need to say exactly what I'd do with those books when my eye fell on them, after all. I silently resolved to move them upstairs, later.

His face lit up. "Thanks!"

"I don't care if it's haunted; rent is $50 a week and we can deal with the ghost later."

I was getting used to overhearing odd conversations in the bookshop, but this one caught my ear. The speakers were a pair of tall, lanky people who I'd suspect of being elves if I hadn't set up wards against them. No-one benefitted from fae glamours when trying to buy books, so losing a little custom was worth the wards—plus, unlike the difficult-to-achieve vampire wards, anti-glamour wards only required a few quartz crystals.

"I don't know," said the skinnier of the pair, worry wrinkling her forehead. Maybe not an elf then – I was sure elves didn't allow wrinkles to mar their appearance. "We didn't manage to get rid of the poltergeist at the last house."

The shorter of the two waved a hand airily. "That was then. Before this bookshop was open again. Besides, $50 a week for an apartment in this town? There's no way we're passing that up." She turned confidently towards me. I stood up hastily;

I'd been trying to reshelve books while keeping an eye on the counter.

The less skinny of the two strode towards me with an authoritative step. "What have you got on exorcism?"

If customer service ethics had allowed me to roll my eyes, I would have done. If a simple exorcism would work, I was betting that the landlord would have got someone in to perform it in a trice. As it was, I couldn't let these customers go without some kind of warning. If they'd already failed to shift a poltergeist (a relatively simple spirit to move on), then anything more difficult was sure well beyond them.

"Please make sure you get a trained professional to assess that apartment before you put any money down," I suggested as I wrapped the book the pair chose. As a friendly local magic bookdealer, making the suggestion was all I could do.

Chapter Sixteen

WIZARDS AND WANDS

The next week, the wizard who'd made a scene in the bookshop asked me out. I accepted, mostly out of curiosity. I wanted to know what made someone want to become a wizard, but not want to take the usual steps to do so. I was also feeling starved for company. Talking to customers all day long wasn't the same as making friends. Even my semi-regular trips to the noodle house and the secondhand shop (not to mention definitely-only-once-a-week early-morning dashes to the bakery) only netted me more customer-retailer conversations, even if I was the customer in those transactions.

It didn't take me long to regret my decision.

"I'm not saying the pigeon's spying on us, but it hasn't blinked in three hours."

My eyes slid over to assess the pigeon in question. A snort escaped me.

"I'm not surprised," I told the would-be wizard. He'd accompanied me to the park after I'd closed the bookshop for the day. I'd been happy to see the white paint on the sign had been washed off at some point. "For a start, we've only been here an hour. For a second, I saw you muttering at it. Did you mean to turn it to stone?"

A blush reddened the few bits of his skin that weren't covered by a scraggly beard.

"No..."

I lifted an eyebrow at my companion.

His blush deepened. "I was trying for cheese."

I stood up, brushing twigs and grass off my linen trousers. I'd had enough of this outing. Lonely or not, I could do better for company.

"You'd better change it back right now. I prefer my pigeons alive. Not stone, not cheese."

The wizard fumbled around in the grass for his wand, but didn't find it. Over by the duck pond where we'd thrown oats to grateful ducks earlier, a dog barked happily and picked up a stick its owner had just thrown. Or no, not exactly a stick, I realised, as sparks flew out of one end and the dog turned rainbow colours. Someone must have picked up the wand thinking it was an innocent bit of tree.

"You'd better go retrieve your wand." It wasn't a suggestion. The wizard scrambled to his feet and ran off towards the dog, who promptly ran in the opposite direction. I sighed. I'd have to hang around to make sure he restored the pigeon to health—after he'd sorted out the dog.

His ethics seemed lax enough that there was no telling whether he'd do so without being watched over. Perhaps that's why he wasn't going through university; they tended to be pretty strict on the ethics side of things.

On the way home I saw a sign hanging at the end of a driveway advertising a bike for sale. *Wheels.* Not having to wait for a bus anytime I wanted to go somewhere sounded like a wonderful idea. I pressed the call button to stop the bus, leaving the protesting wizard behind. I got off the bus and walked back to the driveway.

A few minutes later, I was the proud owner of an ebike. I rode slowly home, getting the hang of the bike and avoiding the ever-present traffic whenever I could. I wheeled it awkwardly through the bookshop and up the stairs to my apartment, where it took up entirely too much space in my living room. Still, it wasn't as though I was entertaining.

The following day, I rode my bike to the closer beach in the sunny evening, not wanting to be subject to the whims of bus timetables or grumpy dwarves. Also, there was no fare for riding my bike, so I saved money, too. While Ron and Kath hadn't mentioned rent, there was bound to be some due. Whenever that happened, I needed to be ready for it, and I didn't want to blow my savings on rent any more than I'd wanted to spend all my cash on temporary accommodation.

I'd anticipated sharing the small beach with other people, given the golden summer evening, but surprisingly, there was no-one around. However, a set of prints led from the water. The owner of the prints was nowhere to be seen. Oddly, they only seemed to come out of the water. There was no corresponding track leading in. Perhaps they'd swum around from the nearby wharf, or from the next bay over.

I shrugged off my outer clothes, leaving on my swimsuit, and headed for the water. I'd timed it right this time, and the sun had warmed the shallow water just enough to make wading into it pleasurable, rather than an exercise in resilience. The westering sun gilded each small, rippling wave and lit up the last few red flowers on the pōhutukawa trees that lined the sandy bay as though they were solstice lanterns. I reached a sufficient depth to swim, and rolled over onto my back, basking in the glorious evening. If every day in the city was like this—not only the sunlit swim, but I'd also sold several books during the day, earning my relaxing evening—then I'd surely made the right decision in coming to the city.

That was when a hand gripped my ankle.

Chapter Seventeen

LEPRECHAUNS AND LETTERS

I reacted automatically, shrieking and splashing for the shore as any sane person would.

Whoever, or whatever, had grabbed me let go as soon as I started kicking. I made it to the shallows without further incident, but before I'd reached the safety of the shore, a silvery tail swirled in front of me, knocking me down. I caught myself on my hands, thankful that the water was still deep enough that I wasn't hurt by the fall, then lurched upright as a bigger than average wave broke around me.

A water-drenched head popped up beside me, blue-green eyes dancing with glee.

"Got you that time."

I rolled my own eyes. Looked like I'd need to read up on mermaids and naiads when I got home. And this time, when I thought of home, I thought of the bookshop.

Fortunately, the water dweller let me go once I'd promised to return for a longer chat.

There was a letter on the mat of the bookshop again the next morning. I picked it up warily, half-expecting another letter from my sister, or maybe even my parents, but the letter was addressed 'to the one who remembers,' and I didn't recognise the handwriting.

While I'd had a lifetime of trying to remember facts and statistics in order to make better predictions, I really didn't think I fitted the description on the label. Unfortunately, neither did any of my customers that day. At least it made a good conversation starter.

"Oh yes," one old woman said to me. "My sister always wanted me to remember cake recipes. But I never could. That's why I buy recipe books. I take photos of the best recipes and work from them. She never guesses the recipe I use isn't in my head." She gave me a sly grin, and waved the book she was about to purchase at me. "Can I have that in a bag, dear?"

I took the book from her—it was titled "Cakes for all Seasons" and had a picture of a cake in the shape of a tree on it, with icing leaves in autumnal colours. As I checked the cover for a price, the leaves changed to a light spring green.

"Nice cover," I commented, wondering who had imbued the book with the changing pictures—and slipped it into one of the paper bags I'd ordered from a local stationery supplier after one too many customers expressed disappointment in my lack of bags for books. I had a plan to make a sticker for the bags one of these days. The only question was whether I should include a hamster on the sticker, or not. Maybe I should split the difference and order half with a hamster, half without. Just as soon as I had figured out how to make the sticker design the right size. My degrees in maths were being put through a workout after shopping hours with *that* exercise.

"I'm good at remembering things," came a familiar voice from below the counter. I peered over. Sure enough, it was the leprechaun. The grimoire's warning about the leprechaun rang in my ears, so when I'd finished the recipe book transaction, I approached with more caution than I otherwise would have done.

"What sort of things do you remember?" I asked him.

> *"Oh, raindrops and rainbows*
> *And buckets of gold*
> *Mining and finding*
> *My heart has grown cold"*

For a moment I'd thought the leprechaun had moved away from rhymes, but it was not to be. The mention of mining tallied with the grimoire's caution about gold, although I was less sure about the reference to his cold heart. *Were* leprechauns cold-hearted? I didn't think that was what the lore said about them. All the same, I changed the subject hastily.

"Did you still want an audiobook?" I asked. "And I did find some maps." I'd carefully removed any maps that showed the shop, after the grimoire's caution. Though I'd only moved them as far as my apartment. Still, any maps that remained in the shop, I didn't mind this leprechaun finding.

> *"Oh glowing moon of my delight*
> *The end is now in sight*
> *I'll tarry not along the way*
> *That right here near the bay*
> *I may stay."*

Well, that didn't answer my question, nor ease my concerns, either. Although I did wonder if the leprechaun and the grimoire might appreciate each others' poems. I resolved to keep an eye on him, but move on to other customers. I still wasn't sure what to do with the letter, but as it was my shop it had been delivered to, I should probably open it. I made sure to walk well away from the leprechaun before I did so. I didn't like the way his eyes followed me. And he didn't ask for either books *or* maps.

It turned out to be a letter for the grimoire, from Kath.

I know you'll be sad at being left behind this time, she wrote. *So I'm sending your new owner on a quest to find you a companion volume.*

She was, was she? It was the first I'd heard of it, and I wondered at the odd, sideways method she'd used to let me know. Still, a companion volume sounded like a good idea. All I had to do was find a rival establishment that might sell me such a thing—because I knew for a fact that none of the books I'd unearthed in this bookshop had cheered up the grimoire. Even the regular company of the vamp, who'd taken to sitting and reading beside it most days, had failed to bring it out of the doldrums. I'd begun to wish that Kath had taken the grimoire with her, no matter how heavy and inconvenient it was to lug around. Still, no doubt she and Ron had enough on their plate with an easily bored djinn for company.

"I don't think it's technically kidnapping if the goldfish follows you home voluntarily."

The speaker was tall and willowy, with a kind of fluid grace that failed utterly to match her words. I was fairly sure she was one of the large dryad community this city boasted. She probably had links to some sort of tree that lived by water, based on the conversation I was eavesdropping on. She was arguing with a short man—or possibly dwarf, given the leather armour which was most of what

I could see from my position at the counter. Or maybe a gnome. I couldn't see the trademark dwarven axe on this customer's back. It definitely wasn't the dwarf from the bus the other night.

"How can a fish follow you?" The leather-clad customer put his hands on his hips, and probably glared too, but I couldn't see his face. I quietly edged around a bookshelf so I could see both speakers. Ah, a gnome. I wondered why he was arguing fish with a dryad. It seemed to me to be an argument that neither party was equipped to win.

"It's easy enough. My stream joins its pond when the rainfall is heavy enough. The thing is, I'm used to its company now. I don't want to take it back." The willowy woman looked down at her hands, as though contemplating a long and lonely life without her goldfish.

"Well, get me another fish for my pond." The gnome's eyes bulged apoplectically.

The woman tucked her flowing dark hair behind one ear. "And if that one follows me home too?"

"Well, then you'd better have a fish ladder installed so it can get back to *my* pond. Or get a breeding colony or something."

"But I'm not good at building things."

"Perhaps I can help," I interjected. "I have books on the care and husbandry of goldfish. But they're not supposed to be released into waterways, so perhaps a native species would be better in your pond?" I turned to the gnome, raising my eyebrows hopefully.

"I'd rather have a frog," he muttered.

"You shouldn't release those either." If his eyes bulged any more, I might have to call in an optician. "Never mind, I'll just show you both to the water care section," I muttered. "This way."

After showing them the books on fish and frogs (not to mention salamanders, cucumber-loving kappa, freshwater kraken and other assorted supernatural water creatures that almost certainly shouldn't be released in our vulnerable islands), I beat a hasty retreat, leaving them deep in an argument on which species was more likely to stay in the gnome's pond. That gnome didn't want to hear about rules. It was a good thing I was just in the business of providing information, not law enforcement.

The streetlights were still lighting the darkness outside when thunderous music from downstairs awoke me.

I rolled over and pulled a pillow over my head. I'd been working hard, on my feet all day yesterday. Why was the grimoire making this racket now?

The volume of the music increased along with the tempo, the strains of Peer Gynt's '*Hall of the Mountain King*' reverberating through the wooden floorboards of the apartment.

"All right, I'm coming," I muttered. I felt around for a cardigan so as to feel more dressed—it wasn't cold enough for one otherwise—and stumbled down stairs.

I paused in disbelief when I reached the last stair.

A battle royale was taking place inside my bookshop. The grimoire was glowing bright blue near the back of the bookshop, so I could see everything clearly, but tinged with a surreal hue.

The dwarf from the bus was standing in the middle of the shop, legs bent in a warrior stance, clutching his axe. His eyes bulged, a ferocious expression on his face. I'd thought him grumpy on the bus, but now he was clearly irate. He was glaring at the leprechaun, who stood beside a hole in the floorboards, right beside the cash register. The boards were not broken, but neatly sawed. The leprechaun had either just climbed out of, or was about to climb into, the hole. My startled glance took in the bucket in his hand. Surely he wouldn't have been able to hold that bucket so lightly if it was full of the gold that leprechauns legendarily sought?

The dwarf didn't seem to notice me. He spun in a fast circle, axe held in both hands, before releasing it. The axe flew across the room, narrowly missing the leprechaun, who ducked in time to save his head but not his hat. The hat rolled off to lie beside the hole in the floorboards. The axe thudded into the wooden bookcase behind it, just missing the books themselves. Splinters flew.

The leprechaun flung some sort of rainbow-coloured magic at the dwarf, who ducked as he sprinted across the room to retrieve his axe. Rainbow-coloured flames roared up in a sheet of fire across the recipe section.

I ran for the grimoire.

"What do I do about this?" I muttered fiercely at it.

The grimoire opened itself up and I scanned the page.

Fool's gold
Takes fae's fancy.

Apparently the grimoire was back to being obscure. Well, I was getting used to that and could make some informed guesses. The leprechaun was arguably a fae of some kind. And dwarves were known for their love of gold. As were leprechauns. So which of them was the problem? No question really; they both were, at this time of night, or rather, early morning. I realised I'd better rephrase the issue. Which of the two intruders was *more* of a problem? No, I still didn't have an answer. But as the dwarf retrieved his axe and limbered up for another swing, and the leprechaun's fingers began to glow like rainbows again, I decided that I just needed to stop them both before they ruined my bookshop.

I still had the brownie's gold upstairs. I'd tried handing it over to the bank along with the rest of the currencies, but they hadn't been keen to accept it, so I'd taken the traditional under-the-mattress approach to banking for that hoard. It hadn't vanished yet. Perhaps *that* 'fae gold' would take their fancy—or at least get them to stop fighting long enough to sort things out.

Shoving the grimoire back into its place—I was beginning to trust it to protect itself by now—I raced upstairs again, my feet driven by the ever-increasing speed of the music. Feeling under my mattress for the coins was tricky to do in a hurry, and I ended up just lifting the entire mattress up to grab the bag that held them.

Then I flew downstairs, the music rising in a crescendo. I flung the coins across the floor. One fell into the hole, but the rest tinkled gently as they hit the floorboards and rolled. The leprechaun leaped for the coins, managing to get his hands on one a moment before the dwarf did the same. Eyes bulging in outrage, the dwarf dived for the leprechaun and caught him by the nape of the neck. They rolled across the floor, tousling each other for the coins and knocking books off the shelves.

Fury darkened my vision for a moment—or no, that was just the grimoire powering down its glow, now that I'd arrived. All the same...

"You are *not* welcome to enter my shop through the floor, throw axes, or *burn books!*" It was easy to put enough outrage in my words that the leprechaun—and the dwarf—would take me seriously. "Put down your weapons and *explain* yourselves!" The '*Hall of the Mountain King*' reached a climax with a final ringing orchestral chord, and stopped.

I hastily turned to the recipe books to try and swat the rainbow fire out, but it vanished as quickly as it had come. Just as well. The whole bookshop was something of a fire hazard. I wondered grimly if I had insurance for this sort of thing. Replacing books and fixing the floor would put a huge dent in my profit margin.

"This little so-and-so interfered with my den," the dwarf growled. "I caught him enlarging it after my axe-throwing—"

"Session?" I finished his sentence.

"Aye. And when I saw him disappear into a crack in the wall, I followed. He'd dug a tunnel all the way along the street to your shop, miss!"

The 'miss' threw me for a moment; it wasn't the way I expected to be addressed by a dwarf, but then I nodded briefly and turned to the leprechaun.

"Your turn."

The leprechaun giggled nervously and picked up his hat, which he wrung in his hands.

"Er—ahaha.

> *'Twas only gold that I seek*
> *Deep under the street.*"

"Under the street is one thing. In my shop is quite another. I'm barring you from entry from now on. And that includes entry by tunnel, understand? If you need gold, you'll have to find it elsewhere. Audiobooks, too." Was it only my imagination that the latter made the leprechaun's shoulders droop? Too bad. I'd have happily sold him maps and audiobooks, but tunnelling into my shop was way beyond acceptable.

Looking at the dwarf, I added, "I don't want to see *you* coming through the floor, either. My books could have been seriously damaged by your axe, and my bookcase *was*. So, thank you for apprehending this intruder, but if you want to return, come through the front door."

"I'm not much of a reader, but I'll bear it in mind." The dwarf succeeded in pulling his axe free, and gave a low bow. "I can recommend a top-notch woodworker for your repairs, mind you."

"Thank you, I'll take it under advisement," I said tartly. I wouldn't have needed bookcase repairs if his axe hadn't damaged it. No wonder he knew a woodworker, I thought glumly. No doubt he often needed one. "Now, everyone out. Bookshop hours start *much* later in the morning."

After the leprechaun and the dwarf both slunk out the front door, I locked it firmly, then sank down to sit on the stair, barely noticing when the grimoire switched the music to Tchaikovsky's '*March Slave*'.

"How on earth can I sleep now?" I murmured, looking from the splintered bookcase to the hole in the floor. There was no answer from anyone.

Chapter Eighteen

THE WEREWOLF

The first customer at the door the next morning was Dirk. He wore a skintight black t-shirt and somewhat looser jogging pants, and held a grocery bag, this time filled with carrots, and a takeaway cup. He thrust the latter at me without saying anything, and it was only my automatic grasp of the cup that stopped it from slipping to the floor when he let it go.

"Er, thanks," I said, my voice still raspy from lack of sleep. I'd pushed a bookcase over it, then crawled into bed for a couple of hours of rest

while I considered what to do. Fix the floor, obviously. But how? I took a sip from the cup, still on autopilot. The freshness of lemongrass and green tea cut through my sleep-deprived haze. It was the morning I would usually have gone to the bakery for treats and a hot drink. Had Dirk noticed my absence? He often turned up there when I did. "Um, thanks again. I needed that." Not that I'd known lemongrass-green tea existed until a moment ago. I took a second, longer sip, then looked around at the mess in the bookshop, and sighed. "I'm not sure that I can open today," I said apologetically, with a wave at the hole. I'd opened the door to Dirk on autopilot, but I should probably have just put up the 'closed' sign.

Dirk peered past me, eyes narrowed. He sniffed deeply a couple of times; not in an 'I've got a cold' way, but in a 'let me test this scent' manner. At least, I thought there was a difference. I supposed that was normal for werewolves.

"Intruders?" he asked. His voice was almost as raspy as mine.

"Yeah." I put the cup on top of a bookshelf for a moment and rubbed my eyes. "A leprechaun got in through the floor. I think he was looking for gold, but a dwarf followed him in. I woke up when they were battling it out down here." I let another sigh escape my lips. "I haven't been robbed, but I *have* been left with an almighty mess."

Someone knocked at the door and Dirk whipped around towards it. An honest-to-goodness growl emanated from his throat. My hair stood on end. That was a primeval, 'I'll kill whatever comes near' growl. Whoever it was flinched away and retreated at speed. I didn't blame them. The room full of books felt as though it had returned to its original forest form in that moment. Anything that stepped inside would surely be prey for the wolf. I had a moment of wild fear. What predator had I invited inside? Maybe I should keep some defensive weapon on hand.

There was a puff of air and the vampire bat appeared in the air between us. Perhaps it was only surprise that made Dirk leap into the air, hands outstretched to catch it, fur sprouting on his bare arms. The bat flitted sideways and out the door again.

Dirk patted me on the shoulder, making me jerk back in startlement. A puppy-dog look entered his eyes for a moment, but then he lifted a finger.

"Macro recipes," he said. Then he pointed at the hole. "Pack can fix."

It took me a minute to work out what he wanted, but then I nodded my thanks.

"Macro recipes, coming right up. Fortunately I don't think the books were completely destroyed by whatever the leprechaun threw at them." I closed the shop door and led the way around the hole to rifle through the books. I found a stack of raw vegetarian recipe books, and added the cookbook with the picture of a whale on it for good measure. "Here you go. On the house, they smell of smoke." I wished now I'd done more than just throw the leprechaun and dwarf out. But then, what else could I have done? Given them a dodgy prophecy?

Dirk grinned, showing his long canines. "Thanks."

Later, a couple of werewolves I'd never seen before appeared with some new floorboards and carpentry tools. They were in and out in an hour, leaving a smooth new piece of flooring behind them, and a sanded bookcase too. They waved off my offer of a book apiece, and also refused payment. "Dirk cooks better from recipe books," one of them assured me.

The vampire appeared again after lunch when a heavy squall washed over the city, bringing a brief period of darkness.

"What interesting exploits you have," he said, examining the new section of floor. He tapped the bookcase which held the recipe books—an area of the bookshop which he usually never spent time in. Daylight had shown me that while some of the books were still saleable, a rainbow swirl of colour decorated the bookcase. It had stayed in place even where the werewolves had sanded it. "A spot of leprechaun magic, too? Hmm. Yes, I see." He turned his smile on me and I took a step backwards. "Still, it seems to be adequately fixed. I do believe I will keep coming here."

"Oh. Good." It was hard to keep up my customer service smile sometimes.

Later, he bought 'A Compendium of Fae', and the Aubergine book. I decided that on balance it was best not to ask why.

Chapter Nineteen

THE VAMPIRE HUNTER

The man standing in the doorway of the bookshop, two hours before opening time, adjusted his trench coat and pushed his dark glasses onto his forehead, where they sat like a second pair of eyes. The gesture revealed his own steely grey eyes which had an intense, gimlet stare. I wished he'd put his sunnies back on properly.

"I suppose you want identification?" he asked in a gravelly voice.

"Well, yes, actually." I crossed my arms over my chest and tried to look as though I asked for ID every day. I was a little disappointed when he reached into his black trench coat—which was totally overdressed for the light drizzle the day had brought, if totally in keeping with current city fashion as I'd observed it—and whipped out a photo ID card. I'd hoped he was just some layabout masquerading as a detective, but apparently not. I suppressed a groan. The last thing I needed was an investigation after the fracas last week. I examined the card closely.

"So you're a building inspector?" My heart sank. Had someone told the council about my repaired floor? Was there some arcane piece of building code that was now non-compliant as a result of the werewolf pack's repairs?

"Ah, no." He rummaged in another pocket and presented me with a second ID. This one said he worked as a detective for Paranormal Police, an organisation I only knew of slightly. That wasn't so bad, I decided. I was sure I wasn't contravening any paranormal laws. It was the mundane ones that were tricky.

I widened my eyes as I looked at him; I'd learnt over the last couple of weeks that looking startled and innocent made people think you probably knew less about the world than they did, and that they'd then explain themselves. Sometimes in annoying words of one syllable, but it was still quite effective.

"I'm looking for a renegade vampire."

If someone had come to the shop two weeks ago with a statement like that, I'd have ushered them in immediately and shown them the nook where the vamp often sat reading to the grimoire. Two weeks ago, I'd been setting anti-vamp wards. To be sure, I hadn't removed those wards—nor would I. But I'd grown a little less wary of the vamp after he'd spent the whole of those two weeks reading aloud the most boring treatises in the shop. It helped that he hadn't even looked sideways at me or my customers. Well, apart from Dirk. And he'd bought books on a regular basis. I could forgive a lot for that.

"I suppose you'll have to keep looking then," I said. "There are none in here." I wasn't lying; he only showed up during opening hours, thank goodness. "I take precautions." I pointed at the plaited string of garlic bulbs I'd rigged up over the door. It didn't seem to stop the vamp from entering, but then, he had permission. I *did* hope it would deter other vamps. If not, well, I had some garlicky meals in my future. Besides, the vamp was far from the only dubious customer I had visit my bookshop. The cactus witch had revisited the shop several times, looking for more spell books of the darker persuasion. I'd directed her towards less harmful tomes whenever I could get away with it. I wasn't convinced she was the type of person I wanted as a regular. At least her foe, the Chaldean scorpion man, hadn't returned. No doubt there were all sorts of unsavory elements in a city this size. In the shop, the grimoire started playing a song about vampire hunters. Was it trying to cue me in on something? Perhaps it was best that I didn't co-operate *too* much with this unknown quantity with his multiple business cards. Unbidden, the memory of dripping white paint on a sign popped into my head. "I don't know if it's relevant, but there was some sort of painted warning at the park down by the motorway. Maybe you should check that out?"

The Paranormal Police detective, or as I suspected he really was, part-time vampire hunter, walked off with several disappointed backward glances. I waited in the shop door until he was well and truly gone.

The next Saturday brought a deluge of rain. Customers trickled in for a couple of hours, then the trickle died away in inverse proportion to the heaviness of the rain. After two hours with not a single customer, not even a werewolf, I decided to close the shop early and go exploring instead.

I didn't feel like swimming in the rain, so I walked to the bus stop, thinking to explore another part of the city. I could have taken my bike, but it looked far too wet for riding. Perhaps I could find another magical bookshop in which to search for a companion volume for my lonely grimoire. I felt bad that I hadn't managed to solve that problem yet. Although running the bookshop *did* take up a lot more energy than I'd expected. No wonder Ron and Kath had been ready to retire, if they'd been keeping it going for years.

A hooded, cloaked stranger sat at the bus stop, folding paper on the only available seat. I stood watching for a while, unsure of protocol. Should I try to find space beside him? Leave the bus-stop and find another? The stranger folded a last few paper edges and held up a paper crane as though to admire it. He glanced at me, and whispered,

"It works only once; choose carefully."

I looked at the man uncertainly. I'd never seen anyone fold paper so fast. And what was I supposed to be choosing? He smiled enigmatically, then placed the paper crane on the sliver of seat beside him. A large, dark blue bus roared up, and I checked the number displayed in its front window. If I remembered the route numbers correctly—and I was certain I did, years of maths had given me a good memory for that sort of thing—this was *not* the bus to the bigger mall in another suburb that should have been arriving now. I checked the time on my phone. The bus I'd planned to take to investigate a potential bookshop was over half an hour late already. When I glanced back, the paper-folding man had disappeared, presumably onto the bus I didn't want to take. He'd left the paper crane on the seat, and I picked it up, thinking to return it to him. As I held it towards the bus, its doors slammed shut and it took off with a puff of warm air.

A solitary bike rider whizzed past, water shooting up from the back wheel, drenching his trousers. Rain dripped off the rider's helmet and scraggly beard. I was surprised to recognise the wizard who'd so disastrously taken me to the park. He hadn't owned a bicycle then. He didn't stop, intent on dodging the rocks which mysteriously flung themselves in his path. I wondered if he'd purchased the cursed bicycle belonging to the teen witch's brother. Those witches had been regular customers up until today, checking out runestones, new tarot decks, even agitating for crystal balls. Almost anything other than actual books, in fact. Still, they weren't the only ones who were interested in book-adjacent purchases, which had encouraged me to spend a little money on investing in new stock. Carefully, a bit at a time, since I couldn't See if my investments would bear fruit. I was reasonably sure they and their friends would be back another day, after the rain eased. If my surmise about the wizard's bike's origins was correct, I should definitely take care to stay on-side with the witches and their family.

Holding the paper crane, I pondered for a moment. *Do I really need to go elsewhere to shop?* I hadn't actually located another appropriate bookshop (no wonder mine was so popular). Going out could be a fool's mission. But if I didn't take the bus somewhere... I could save the money and visit my favourite bakery. Maybe even order some takeaway Thai for dinner. That decided it for me.

I tucked the paper crane into my bag and turned my steps towards the corner bakery. If I hurried, there might still be a cherry cream choux pastry with my name on it. And if I ate it in one sitting, there was no chance that the hamsters could take a share.

I *had* purchased actual hamster food. At least, I had bought pellets formulated for rats, and added extra grains in a couple of small dishes: one in the kitchen, one in the lounge. With no hamsters legally in the country, it was no wonder that real hamster food wasn't readily available. The server in the pet shop had given me quite a lecture when I asked for it.

Still, I felt as though I might be starting a rat problem, so I set traps beside the food, too. Hopefully hamsters which somehow made it through the strict biosecurity protocols that kept our islands free from unexpected imports would be smart enough to avoid rat traps. But just in case, the traps I had installed were designed for live capture. Goodness knew what I'd do if I actually caught a hamster. If I contained one, would I then be obliged to report it? Maybe it was best if the question didn't arise.

Chapter Twenty

THE GRIMOIRE

Monday morning brought a cessation of rain, and not one, but two packages. The first package arrived wrapped in yesterday's newspaper, but it was postmarked three decades in the future. I picked it up and recognized my Dad's handwriting. How typical of my Seer family, to not only get my address before I knew it myself, but to be confident enough in their predictions that they'd send something which couldn't be used for years. My fingers brushed over the stamped date. Of course, I could open it early. What would happen to their predictions and plans then? But I took the paper-wrapped packet upstairs and set it on the desk that took up one corner of my new living room. I was sure that they'd have *Seen* if I opened it or not, and taken precautions accordingly. It wasn't worth a potential ward-breaking and/or practical joke (if Delphine had been involved) to open the package, no matter how it plucked at my curiosity. I sighed. It plucked at my still-present homesickness, too. How was it possible that I could feel homesick, while simultaneously being full of optimism and plans for my new future *away* from home? Shaking my head at my inner conflict, I placed the paper crane on top of the package as a combination of decoration and memory-aid. I'd looked up the significance of paper cranes last night, and found they were said to be symbols of hope, peace or healing. I could use any of those things. The paper crane deserved a place of honour. The desk was the best I could do.

The second package was wrapped in plastic. It bore my sister's writing and no odd dates. It was heavy, and nothing rattled when I shook it. This one, I opened. Inside was a note, slipped into the pages of a startlingly familiar looking grimoire, complete with ornate Celtic scrollwork on the cover, and a small 'II' under that.

I pulled out the note and read.

Dear Sibyl,

I See you are enjoying your new home. Keep an eye on that werewolf, he's bound to be a good customer one way or another. I can't believe you let the vamp stay. Do you want me to tell Mum about him? She'll freak if I do, but she won't come visit unless you invite her. By the way, I was in Napier last weekend and came across the enclosed book in the most fantastic little bookshop there. It's run by a wizard. I don't think it was there last time we visited, but you know how some of those shops pop in and out of existence. It doesn't look like yours is one of those. Lucky thing really, given you'll be there for a while. I thought this grimoire looked a lot like the one I've Seen you holding, so I knew you'd appreciate it. BTW Rex is having the time of his life with cousin Tim.

Best,

Delphine

Seers. Who'd have them as family? The mention of my dog Rex was a source of both pain and pleasure. *At least he is alive. I wish he was here.* But my sister Delphine had saved me a lot of time and trouble by sending me another grimoire. At least, I hoped she had. After all, I hadn't had much luck with any of the books I'd tried so far. I carried the new grimoire downstairs to the one that already sat in the scrolls nook, and made space for the second volume by rearranging the shelves.

"Look what I've got for you," I said with a smile, gently pushing the new grimoire in next to the old.

The first grimoire flipped itself to the floor and ruffled its pages in excitement. The second one did the same. The two grimoires flapped to and fro like a pair of ungainly butterflies on the bookshop floor before settling down with an air of contentment. And the music player burst forth with song: *Oh Sole Mio*.

I retreated to make myself a cup of tea and get the bookshop ready for opening. It was time to leave the grimoire and its new companion volume to get acquainted. I had a bookshop to run. I'd found a catalogue of recipe books to browse through—given how often Dirk came through and looked at them, those books could be well be my best-selling item. And one weekend soon, I'd try to make friends with the mermaid at the beach. Just not yet. I had to do a lot of research, first. It was a good thing I had plenty of books to hand. As the music faded a little, I unlocked the peeling painted door of the bookshop, ready for whatever surprise the day would bring.

The end.

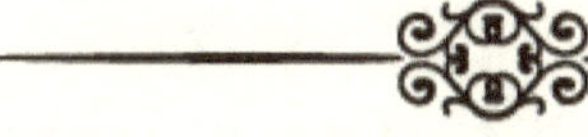

Author's Note

I hope you've enjoyed this cosy urban fantasy novella. If you did, please consider taking the time to leave a review wherever you bought it, or on your favourite review site. It really helps other readers to know if they'd like the book too. And there is more to come in the Woodside series! I've really enjoyed transforming parts of the city where I grew up into a fantastical realm.

I'd like to acknowledge the Writers Cafe Auckland, whose Advent writing prompts provided the impetus and backbone for this story. It was great fun weaving a story around some of the more bizarre ones! Thanks to Anne, Annie and Susy for always making me think, and for your encouragement to keep writing stories, not to mention picking up close repetitions and other errors. Thanks to Keri who also lent her keen eyes to the manuscript, picking up all sorts of things I would have missed. Thanks also to the SpecFicNZ Monday night write club, which helps me to set aside dedicated time to get words on paper. Thank you to Grace for her helpful edits!

And as always, thank you to my family for supporting me to write.

Also by Melissa Gunn

Weather Gods:

Flash Flood

Thunder Snow

Storm Surge

Heat Wave

Woodside Cosy Urban Fantasy:

Divination and Disaster

Seers and Salt

Grimoires and Green Tea

Short stories & novellas:

Treescape (First published in Magic and Mystery: A Limited Edition Urban Fantasy Mystery Anthology)

Feels Like Heaven (in Aftermath: Stories of Survival in Aotearoa New Zealand)

First Pav on Mars (in Pav Deconstructed, Pavlova Press)

A Gift of Coconuts (in Imagine 2200 2024 collection)

Sweet enough? (in Artificial Sweetener: Tales of AI: 100% Written by Humans)

Hauraki Lament or a Song of Love? (in Tales of the Hauraki Gulf)

About the Author

Melissa Gunn always planned to write books, but she trained as a scientist and climbed trees after squirrels first. Melissa enjoys combining facts that seem fantastical with actual fantasy, and creating quirky characters with a sense of humour. When she's not trying to figure out how a dryad would react to the modern world, she takes photographs of whatever will stand still for long enough (mostly plants). She spent several years pursuing a science career before turning to fiction - though it turns out that there is even more research involved. Luckily, research is one of her favourite things.